JUN 2010

Tales from Grace Chapel Inn

Going to the Chapel

Rebecca Kelly

Guideposts

CARMEL, NEW YORK

Acknowledgments

All Scripture quotations, unless otherwise noted, are taken from
The Holy Bible, New International Version. Copyright © 1973,
1978, 1984 International Bible Society. Used by permission of
Zondervan Bible Publishers.

Scripture quotations marked (KJV) are taken from
The King James Version of the Bible.

"America," lyrics by Samuel Francis Smith (1808–1895).

www.guidepostsbooks.com

Series Editors: Regina Hersey and Leo Grant
Cover art by Edgar Jerins
Cover design by Wendy Bass
Interior design by Cindy LaBreacht
Typeset by Composition Technologies, Inc.
Printed in the United States of America

# Acknowledgments

I would like to thank Lorraine Martindale for creating the marvelous characters and places in the little town of Acorn Hill, and Regina Hersey and Leo Grant for making my first visit there such a delight.

—Rebecca Kelly

Chapter One

Spring had arrived with a burst of color and warmth in the little town of Acorn Hill, Pennsylvania, and now bloomed into glorious May. Sunshine gilded every day, warming the air, coaxing up window shades and dancing in the sparkling water of the little creek just south of town. Lawns turned thick and green, tickling bare feet like lush, cool carpets, while trees became dense with leaves and their branches heavy with ripening fruits and nuts. Even when it rained, the sun only seemed to play hide-and-seek with the clouds before returning to paint the sky a bright, vivid blue.

The gardens at Grace Chapel Inn had likewise become an extraordinary palette of vibrant colors. Black-eyed Susans held up their cheerful orange and brown faces to catch every ray of light, while curly blue irises fluttered, and delicately arched pink lady's slippers danced with every hint of breeze. Purple Asian lilies painted a bolder swath of color, vying with fragrant white lilacs and the lush vines of ruffled blue sweet peas to catch the eye of any passing visitor.

"Come here, you." Jane Howard had to stretch to pluck the last scraggly weed that had invaded the far edge of her bed of jewel-toned pansies. Once she had tugged it from the soil, roots and all, she sat back on her heels and tossed it into her work basket. "There. That's much better."

With her wide-brimmed straw hat and worn blue denim overalls, Jane looked perfectly at home among the flowers. In order to keep cool and tidy while working in the kitchen and garden, she wore her long dark hair pulled back into its usual ponytail. A gold bracelet with little enameled cats jingled on her right wrist as she stood and picked up her work basket.

That should do it for today. She inspected the results with satisfaction. Now that the danger of frost was past, she could transplant some of the seedlings she had started to fill in a few shady spots, but she would have to water more often. She made a mental note to scatter a little wood ash in the vegetable garden; that might discourage the slugs that were creeping out at night to nibble on her brussels sprouts.

When Jane had first come home to Acorn Hill after her father's death, she had worked out much of her grief by taming the overgrown and neglected vegetable and flower gardens. Now they had become a place where Jane could think, daydream or just enjoy the beauty of nature. She divided most of her time between the kitchen and the gardens, and had found that starting cuttings and pulling weeds were just as fulfilling as baking fresh bread or preparing a delicious meal. The pleasure that her efforts gave to others always repaid her in full.

She also felt better about herself when she spent a few hours working outdoors in the fresh air and sunshine. She certainly had no desire to return to the stressful life she had left behind in San Francisco. The wounds left by her divorce and her ex-husband Justin Hinton's attempts to undermine her career as a chef were still very painful. Her decision to stay in Acorn Hill and help her sisters transform their childhood home into an inn had been drastic, even for her, but Jane needed to be around those who truly loved her.

It had been the right thing to do. Now that the inn was up and running smoothly, Jane and her sisters had found a curious sort of harmony with each other. Working together brought with it a sense of unity and purpose, one that filled in the gaps in their lives and brought back a wonderful sense of family and belonging. Jane had not enjoyed feelings like these since her childhood.

And if someone had told me a year ago my biggest worry would be when to plant the begonias and how to chase off pesky slugs, I'd have laughed myself silly, Jane thought. She had been under so much stress at work that it was a miracle she had not snapped. Even away from the restaurant, she had been battered by Justin's excessive jealousy, and then by the wrenching loneliness that he had left in his wake. She had dragged herself through every day, forcing herself to endure what was expected of her. She had almost lost all her sense of hope.

Living here with Louise and Alice was helping to heal all the old wounds, and to leave the unhappiness in the past, where it belonged. Now Jane woke up every morning not dreading the day ahead, but eagerly looking forward to it. She was beginning to see what a good life she could have here, and she wanted that—more than she had ever wanted anything else.

The gardens symbolized her hope for the future, too. For in a garden, there was always the possibility of a fresh start.

"Jane? Are you out here?"

She looked up to see her middle sister Alice hurrying out the side door. "Over here."

"Oh, good." Looking a little harried, Alice came down the path. She was wearing her nurse's uniform, and her bobbed brown hair bounced with every step she took. In her right hand she carried a pale ivory and green glass vase, and a large open basket was hooked over her left arm. "We need fresh flowers for the guest rooms, and Louise is preparing to check out the Winchells. Would you help me cut some?"

There were faint dark shadows under Alice's kind brown eyes, and Jane became concerned. "I can do them myself, if you're late for work."

"That's okay, I have a couple of hours before I have to go in." In addition to helping her sisters run the inn, Alice worked part-time as a ward nurse at the hospital in Potterston. "Besides, you've been out here since lunchtime."

"I've been battling weeds, and the weeds lost. The dreaded leaf-eating slugs are next." Jane picked up her clippers and handed Alice another pair.

The vase her sister carried was one their father used to keep on his desk.

Alice carefully set it down with the basket on a nearby bench. "I need the vase for the parlor. Wendell knocked the blue one off the side table in there and broke it yesterday."

"That spoiled cat thinks every flat surface in this house belongs to him." Jane winced as her sister attacked one of the lilac bushes the same way she would trim a hedge. "Um, try not to cut so many of the new canes, Alice. We need a bucket of water, too."

"Sorry." Alice peered at the bush. "Why do we need a bucket of water when I have the vase?"

"Lilacs wilt really fast if you don't put them in water right away. We can transfer them to the vase once you have just the arrangement you want. Hang on." Jane went over to where she kept the garden hose neatly coiled and filled a small plastic bucket with water, then came back and showed her sister which blooms to cut. "Clip the canes at a slant and put them right in the bucket. You can cut the next one down, too, that's an older one. If you clip the ones that are just starting to bloom, they'll last longer."

"Right." Alice frowned and selected the next blossom with greater care. "Is that why the lilacs you cut always seem to last longer than mine?"

"That and my top-secret gardener's trick. I don't get the

florets wet—they don't like water—and I sprinkle a little flower food in the vases." Jane sorted through several stems before finding one ready to cut, then handed it to Alice. "Lilacs are fussy flowers."

Her sister carefully placed it in the bucket. "Maybe you could put something similar to flower food in Rev. Highland's tea."

Jane thought of the minister's stern features. He had been a guest at the inn for the past three days, and every morning had ordered plain tea and toast. "Why? Is he starting to wilt?"

"Oh, no." Alice assured her. "I was . . . I was only kidding."

"Then what? Doesn't he like my tea?"

"No, it's just . . ." She glanced around, then lowered her voice. "This is very confidential, Jane—you know you can't repeat what I tell you, not to anyone."

Alice served as a member of the church board for Grace Chapel, and was involved in interviewing candidates to be the church's new head pastor. It was a bittersweet process, as their father had served as head pastor of Grace Chapel for more than fifty years before his death. Over the years, Daniel had also become the heart of their small, quiet community, and his loss had left everyone in Acorn Hill feeling more than a little bewildered.

Alice was quite serious about her position on the board, so Jane nodded. "I promise, I won't breathe a word."

"Thanks. The truth is, Rev. Highland doesn't really like *anything*." Her sister released a heavy sigh. "The board conducted the interview with him yesterday, and while his resumé and qualifications are very impressive, he's a man of very . . . strong opinions."

Jane had seen Rev. Highland earlier, but as was his custom, he spent the morning brooding over the newspaper and saying little. "What sort of strong opinions?"

"You name it, he has a strong opinion on it. During his interview, he told the board that engaged couples should be required to take weekly classes in spiritual instruction and marital counseling."

Jane frowned. "That's not all that unusual. A lot of churches offer that for young couples."

"Every week for an entire year prior to the wedding?"

"Ouch." She winced. "That is tough."

"And that's not the worst of it. When Mayor Tynan asked him about his views on divorce, he stated that anyone who divorces and then remarries is, in his opinion, living in sin."

"Oh, dear."

"Exactly. He even quoted from the book of Matthew."

Alice looked over her shoulder at the second-floor windows. "He has the right amount of experience and certainly the background, but with that attitude. . . ." she shook her head.

Jane thought of her own brief marriage to Justin Hinton. She had no desire to remarry—or even to date, for that matter—but she certainly would not want to be labeled as sinful if she did. "The board wouldn't really hire someone like that, would they, Alice?"

"Good Lord, no." Her sister turned back to the bush and snipped off another fluffy white bunch. "People need a minister who will help them with whatever trouble they have in their lives, not kick them out of the church for it."

That made Jane's heart feel a little lighter. "It might help if you could get a minister with a gentler viewpoint, someone who is more in step with modern times."

"We can't offer candidates a high salary," Alice admitted. "Money isn't the main problem, though. We've already interviewed several prospects, most of whom were quite suitable, but the board can't agree on anyone. It doesn't look like we'll find a replacement for Father any time soon."

That explained the shadows under her sister's eyes. Jane knew how difficult it was for her sister to deal with this

particular task—of Daniel's daughters, Alice had been clos-
est to their father and had taken his death the hardest. The
fact that the board was at odds over whom to hire would also
worry Alice, who tended to avoid conflict whenever possible.

On impulse Jane reached over and gave her sister a one-
armed hug. "Don't worry about it. I'm sure there's a perfect
minister for Grace Chapel out there somewhere. It's just a
matter of time before he shows up and you hire him." The
sound of a car pulling up the drive made her chuckle.
"Maybe that's him now."

Louise Howard Smith added the column of figures in her
ledger for the second time, to check the accuracy of her total,
and lifted the wire-rimmed reading glasses she wore fastened
to a chain around her neck to read the calculator's display.

Louise was the most meticulous and disciplined of
Daniel Howard's daughters. It showed in the precise cut of
her short silver hair and the shrewd gaze of her light blue
eyes. She was also quite practical, as suggested by the comfortable light tan cotton skirt and matching beige pullover
that she wore.

She checked off the total in the ledger book and moved
on to the next column. Her fingers tapped the calculator's
keys with the same blind precision she used to play the piano.
After a lifetime of studying and teaching music, she had
never imagined herself keeping books and running an inn,
but the change was doing her good. She was busy, she was
productive and, most of all, she was not alone anymore.

The four years before she had agreed to run Grace
Chapel Inn with her sisters had been bleak. First she had had
to endure the devastation of losing her dear husband Eliot to
cancer, and then she had been forced to go on without him.
For years she had wandered aimlessly through each day, feeling no sense of direction or meaning. She had occasionally

visited her daughter Cynthia, who was pursuing a career in children's publishing in Boston, but she could not bring herself to intrude further on her child's busy life.

Leaving the home she had shared with Eliot in Philadelphia and moving back to Acorn Hill had been the hardest thing she had done since burying her husband. It was also the best thing she had done, for now her days were filled with activity and satisfaction. She was not only contributing something by helping her sisters to run Grace Chapel Inn, she was rediscovering that part of herself that she thought she had lost along with Eliot.

The sound of the counter bell interrupted Louise's calculations. She suspected that Alice and Jane were still out in the garden, so she turned off her calculator and went out to greet the man and woman standing at the front desk.

The Winchells were a very attractive couple in their late thirties. Rev. Jacob Winchell was of average height and weight, and he had a handsome face and a ready smile. He kept his auburn hair so well groomed that Louise had never seen him with so much as a single hair out of place.

Brynda Winchell stood a few inches shorter than her husband, and still retained much of the beauty and polish that had taken her all the way to becoming a finalist in the Miss Pennsylvania pageant. She was a pleasant woman and quite friendly, although most of her attention was usually centered on her spouse. Her smartly styled brown hair was almost, but not quite, as perfect as her husband's.

"Are you ready to check out?" Louise asked, somewhat wary. Mrs. Winchell had come down several times that morning to postpone their checkout, explaining that her husband was either waiting for an important call or making one. Louise had begun to wonder if she should simply save herself the headaches and book them for another night.

"Yes, if we could, Mrs. Smithers."

Louise eyed him. "It's Mrs. *Smith*."

"Smith. Right." Jacob Winchell frowned as something chimed in his pocket, then took out a cellular phone and walked a short distance away from the desk to answer it. "Yes? On my way, Hugo. We're just wrapping up things here in Chestnut Hill."

Louise suppressed a sigh. Since arriving at Grace Chapel Inn, Rev. Winchell had persisted in calling the town everything from Pecan Hill to Walnut Hill, yet no matter how often she corrected him, he could not seem to remember the actual name.

If he calls our town Peanut Hill, Louise thought, *I may have to leave the room.*

"Hugo is Jacob's personal assistant," Mrs. Winchell said to Louise in a low, confidential murmur. "He arranges all of my husband's public appearances."

"Indeed!" Louise thought it a pity that Hugo couldn't arrange a timely checkout for him. "He must be a very popular . . . speaker?"

"Sometimes I think poor Jake does nothing but speak. He attends at least a dozen conferences and retreats during the year, and then offers free lectures at community colleges, and serves as the keynote speaker at all sorts of luncheons and dinners." The younger woman sighed. "He made so many speeches last year that he lost his voice and had to see a throat specialist. Now he has to gargle three times a day and can't say a word twenty-four hours before he has to appear in public."

Given the husband's obvious affection for his cell phone, Louise guessed that must be utter torture. "How terribly inconvenient," she sympathized.

"He never complains, though." She gave her husband a singularly adoring look. "He truly has the patience of a saint."

And a phone bill of epic proportions, Louise decided.

"About an hour. Yes. Thank you." He ended the call and was about to put the phone away when it rang a second time. He covered the receiver and looked over his shoulder to give

Louise an apologetic smile. "Sorry, things get a bit hectic when I'm away from the office."

"Yes." She looked pointedly at his phone. "I have noticed that."

Rev. Winchell gestured vaguely at the paperwork in Louise's hand. "Uh, honey, would you take care of signing whatever has to be signed so we can get out of here? I want to get on the highway before noon." Without waiting for Brynda's agreement, he was back on the phone.

Louise let out a breath slowly, and then tallied up their bill and handed the charge slip to Mrs. Winchell for her review and signature. "Are you and your husband heading back home?"

"Yes, right away. Jake has just been offered a chance to direct and produce his own community-access television program back in Ohio. He's going to call it *Holy Toledo*." Mrs. Winchell signed her name to the charge slip, then added, "He's planning on doing three half-hour shows a week, then go to a five-day schedule near Christmas."

He'd better start gargling four times a day. "Well, then I guess if he's hired as our head pastor, he'll be calling his program, what? 'Holy Hill?'"

"Oh, that's so funny." She produced a lilting laugh. "I'll have to tell Jake that."

The man was still on the phone. "Do you have to get an appointment from Hugo to do that?"

That made his wife laugh even harder. When she had controlled her mirth, she leaned over the desk and whispered, "We haven't told anyone yet, but I'm afraid Jake won't be able to take the job here. The television program is such a tremendous opportunity for him. You understand how it is."

"Yes, I believe that would be the better choice for him." *It really would.* Louise personally thought Jacob needed to spend less time making speeches and personal appearances, and more time being a minister, but at least he wouldn't be doing it in Acorn Hill. She detached the customer copy of the charge slip and handed it to Mrs. Winchell. "Have a safe trip home, and thank you for staying with us."

"Thank you, Mrs. Smith." Mrs. Winchell beamed before taking her husband's arm and leading him out through the front entrance.

"Good-bye, Rev. Winchell." Louise couldn't help calling out next. "Come back again to Peanut Hill soon."

Still talking on the phone, Rev. Winchell waved without looking back at Louise.

"Maybe I should have asked for an autograph," she murmured, then chuckled at herself and put the signed slip away in the cash drawer. "So much for that one."

Like all the candidates being considered by the church board, Jacob Winchell had given a guest sermon during the previous Sunday's services as part of the interview process. Afterward, Louise had overheard him on his cell phone, complaining to someone about the lighting and the fact the little church didn't have a sound board.

With her usual efficiency Louise finished recording and filing the checkout paperwork for the Winchells. As she put away the last folder, a tall, dark-haired man came in through the front entrance.

"Good afternoon."

"Good afternoon. Welcome to Grace Chapel Inn." Louise noted his immaculate navy blue suit, and the fact that he carried a slim briefcase. A salesman or businessman traveling through the area was her guess. "May I help you?"

"My name is Kenneth Thompson. I have a reservation through Sunday." He had a smooth, pleasant voice with a faint accent that reminded her of the people Cynthia worked with in Boston.

Louise briefly went over the rates and the services they offered their guests.

Kenneth removed a sleek wallet from the inside pocket of

his jacket, and produced a credit card and driver's license. Louise noticed the unusual gold signet ring he wore on his right hand. From the worn scrolled design in the metal she guessed it to be a family heirloom. As she took his card, two more guests came downstairs and greeted them.

"Good afternoon, Mrs. Smith." Trent Alcott, an estate buyer who already had stayed twice at the inn, set down his briefcase. "Do you have any messages for me?"

"No, Mr. Alcott." Louise smiled at the elderly woman beside him. She thought it was charming that Trent always brought his mother with him on his business trips. "Are you and Mrs. Alcott off to another auction?"

"Two or three, if Mother doesn't get too tired." The always friendly and outgoing Trent held out his hand to Kenneth. "How do you do, Trent Alcott from Philadelphia."

He shook his hand. "Kenneth Thompson from Boston. A pleasure to meet you."

"If you're interested in antiques, then you've come to the right place." Trent gestured around the lobby. "The ladies have a real treasure trove here. Notice the hat rack when you came in?"

Kenneth glanced back at the foyer. "Yes, as a matter of fact I did. It's a Thonet bentwood. Nineteenth century, isn't it?"

"It is indeed." Impressed, Trent grinned. "You're a man who knows your antiques." He shot a sideways look at Louise. "I've been trying to talk Mrs. Smith here into selling it to me, but she has so far resisted all my offers, and not just to drive up the price, you understand."

Louise eyed the lovely old rack, which she remembered her father had rescued when a train station in a neighboring town had been renovated. "I'm sorry, Mr. Alcott, but we are rather attached to it."

"That's a shame." Trent walked over and ran an admiring

hand over the gleaming, honey-colored wood. "You don't see many old beech pieces like this in such fine condition."

"It would be worth several hundred dollars to a serious collector," Kenneth told Louise.

She had never considered how much the antiques that Daniel Howard had collected over the years were worth. To her and her sisters, the rack had always represented fond memories of going to meet visiting relatives who had come in on the train.

That Kenneth knew the dollar value of it disturbed her a little. She would have liked it better if he had guessed at the sentimental value of the piece instead. "My, that is good to know."

"What do you say, Mrs. Smith?" The estate buyer came back to the desk and gave her a cajoling smile. "Change your mind, make some money."

Before Louise could formulate yet another polite refusal, Nancy Alcott suddenly took hold of her son's arm and pulled him away. "Come, Trent, we're going to be late."

"Whoops." Trent stumbled over the edge of the reception area rug, turning over one corner. He went to straighten it, but his impatient mother gave him another tug.

"No dawdling," his mother continued as she led him out the front door. "You know how your father feels about punctuality."

After the Alcotts' blue sedan left the driveway, it only took Louise a few minutes to take Kenneth Thompson's credit card information and sign him in. In a small notebook he recorded the amount she was charging and the times breakfast and tea were served.

Louise herself was meticulous, but she thought writing things down in a notebook went a bit overboard. *Well, perhaps he has to file some kind of expense report with his company.*

By the time she was ready to show him to his room, she

heard the side door to the gardens open. "Would you be interested in the local attractions and events in the area?" she asked, reaching for the stack of promotional flyers under the counter.

"I hope to do a little sightseeing while I'm here," Kenneth told her, "but at present I'll be busy with interviewing in town."

"Oh, are you looking for a job?" Louise glanced at her sisters, who were bringing in flowers from the garden. The heady smell of lilacs preceded them.

"I've applied for a position as head pastor for Grace Chapel."

"Oh," Louise said. "Forgive me for not recognizing your name. There are three of us who take reservations."

"I would have been surprised if you had, but I guess I'm not used to small towns . . . yet," he said with a smile. Then he picked up his briefcase and turned just as Alice and Jane walked by the front of the desk.

Moving too quickly and distracted by the sight of their visitor, Alice caught her heel on the upturned edge of the rug and yelped as she lost her balance and pitched forward. Jane grabbed her from behind to keep her from falling, but the vase of flowers Alice was carrying went flying directly at Kenneth.

"Careful!" Kenneth tried to grab the vase, but ended up with two handfuls of white lilac canes instead.

Louise gasped as the delicate glass fell to the floor and smashed into a thousand pieces.

"Oh, no!" Alice cried as her gaze went from the broken glass to Kenneth Thompson's face. She looked absolutely horrified.

"Are you all right?" Kenneth set the flowers on the reception desk before turning to Alice.

"I'm fine, just . . . terribly embarrassed." She tried to work up a smile but her face flushed. "I'm so sorry."

"Please, don't apologize," Kenneth said. "I meant to straighten that rug myself."

"That's okay. We usually don't greet our guests by throwing vases of lilacs at them." Jane set her basket aside and held out her hand. "Welcome to Grace Chapel Inn. I'm Jane Howard, and this lady with the very pink face is my sister, Alice Howard."

"Kenneth Thompson, a pleasure. Again, I'm sorry about the vase." He clasped Jane's hand, then Alice's, and ducked his head to meet her gaze. "Are you sure you're all right, Ms. Howard?"

She took a deep breath and nodded. "Yes, thank you."

Wendell, their father's pampered tabby cat, wandered in from the side parlor. He came over to sniff at a shard of glass and Kenneth's shoe before Alice scooped him up in her arms.

Louise said to her sisters, "Rev. Thompson is here to interview for the position of head pastor."

As her sisters looked at their guest with renewed interest, Louise suggested, "Jane, why don't you show Rev. Thompson up to his room? Alice and I will take care of this."

Her younger sister nodded and led their guest away, while Alice put Wendell on a chair before she bent down and began cautiously gathering shards. "Go ahead and say it, Louise. I should have been more careful."

Louise remembered nagging Alice earlier about the same thing. "I am not saying a word. Not to a nurse who knows that broken vase could have been her knee, or her head."

She went back into the office for the small broom and dustpan she kept in the closet there, and then returned with them and a small trash can. "Although at the rate we're going through vases, we better add them as a line item to the monthly budget."

Chapter ✤ Two

Alice and Louise had just started sweeping up the broken glass when the front door opened and their aunt sailed in.

"I've got a nice little surprise for you, girls," Ethel Buckley called out.

The Howard sisters' aunt was a plump woman with red hair that she kept short. She had pale blue eyes and a lively, expressive face that reflected her energetic personality. The pretty pastel floral dress she wore complemented her hair and fair complexion.

Ethel (the sisters still called her Aunt Ethel) had moved back to Acorn Hill after her husband Bob had died, when she sold their farm and decided to relocate closer to her brother Daniel and his daughters. Since then, she had been living in the carriage house next to Grace Chapel Inn, and often stopped in unannounced to check on her nieces and relate whatever news she had from town. Ethel loved to gossip, and since she had started dating Acorn Hill's mayor, Lloyd Tynan, she had a steady supply of it. But there were times when her unexpected visits were somewhat inconvenient.

What now? Louise thought.

"These are fresh from the—oh, my goodness!" As soon

as she spotted the broken glass, she set aside the covered plate she was carrying and hurried over to Louise and Alice. "What happened?"

"We just had a little accident—no one was hurt." Alice held the dustpan at an angle for Louise as she swept another pile of shards into it. "That smells wonderful, Aunt Ethel." She nodded toward the plate Ethel had brought in. "Did you bake something special for us?"

"My peach tarts, I thought you might like to have them with your tea this afternoon." Ethel bent down to peer at the broken glass, then caught her breath and drew back, shocked. "Oh, my dears. *Please* tell me you didn't smash one of the green cameo vases!"

"I don't know about the cameo part, but it was a green vase," Alice said, shrugging her shoulders, "and it's definitely smashed."

"Oh, Alice." Ethel pressed her hand to her heart, horrified all over again. "If Daniel were here to see this, it would break his heart."

Louise glanced at her aunt with a frown. "I know our father liked to have fresh flowers around the house, Aunt Ethel, but we do have other vases."

"That vase was made from cameo glass, Louise, which hasn't been made since the Depression." She gestured at the shards. "Don't you remember them? Daniel gave a matching pair of those vases to your mother for their second wedding anniversary."

Now that Ethel had jogged her memory, Louise did recall that her mother had kept the vases in her room. "Let us just be thankful no one was hurt."

"Oh, no, I remember now—those were her favorite vases, weren't they?" Alice was staring at the small pile of shards in the trash can as if trying to figure out how to put them back together. "With all our redecorating and rearranging, I'd forgotten about them or I would never have taken it."

"Did you forget how after your mother passed away, Daniel used to keep at least one of them on the desk in his study? You girls used to fill them with flowers from the garden for him," Ethel continued. "He said they reminded him of Madeleine every day." She shook her head. "I can't believe you girls were so careless."

Louise couldn't believe how excellent her aunt's memory was—or how blind she was to Alice's feelings. "It was an unavoidable accident," she said firmly. "Alice was coming in from the garden and she collided with one of our guests."

"Well then, maybe he should pay for the vase," Ethel snapped, still clearly upset. "It's one thing to invite strangers into this house, Louise, but quite another when they start destroying the family heirlooms." She peered around. "Who is this man? Can't he stay somewhere else?"

Alice stood up and straightened her uniform. "The accident was my fault, Aunt Ethel, not his. I wasn't paying attention, I tripped over the edge of the rug and I almost hit the poor man with that vase."

Louise patted her shoulder. "The important thing is that you are all right. Vases are much easier to replace than a knee or a hip."

"I thought I heard your voice, Auntie." Jane came down and went over to give the indignant Ethel a kiss on her cheek. "*Mmm*, you smell like peaches. Are you trying out a new perfume on Mayor Tynan, or have you been snitching fruit from someone's orchard?"

"I brought over some of my peach tarts for your tea." Ethel took the plate and placed it in her niece's hands. "Come, Jane, I'm desperately in need of a cup myself right now."

Alice followed her sisters and aunt into the kitchen, where Jane put on the kettle and Louise set out the cups and saucers on the table.

Seeing their mother's dainty Wedgwood tea service made Alice feel even worse. She had always tried to take care of all the lovely things Madeleine had left behind, not only for her father's sake, but because they were links in a chain of happy childhood memories. How could she have forgotten about the vases?

I was in a hurry and I wasn't thinking, she reminded herself. *Louise is right, I have got to slow down.*

"I noticed that visiting minister and his wife leaving earlier," Ethel said as she sat down and uncovered the plate she had brought. Her tarts were her pride and joy, each one like a perfect miniature pie. The delicious smell of warm fruit blended with the fragrant tea as Jane poured. "Are they on their way back to—where were they from—Ohio?"

"Yes, they just checked out this afternoon," Louise said. "Rev. Winchell seems to be a very busy man."

"I thought they were a nice couple." Alice noticed the way her aunt wrinkled her nose at that. "Didn't you like them?"

"I'm sure they're very nice people, but that sermon he gave at church last Sunday . . . all that walking around and gesturing and smiling like that? *Tsk, tsk!* If I wanted to watch someone act, I'd stay home and turn on the television."

"You might get your chance." Louise told her about Rev. Winchell's personal assistant and his plans for a cable access program. "Perhaps someday we can say, 'We knew him when he did his own hair. . . .'"

"He doesn't, the wife does it for him," Jane said. When everyone looked at her, she grinned. "I walked by their room yesterday morning and heard him telling her to comb in more mousse."

"And he's really going to call this show of his *Holy Toledo?*" Ethel shook her head sadly.

"He was a little, um, theatrical." Alice passed the creamer to Louise and helped herself to a tart. "Going to services is never dull these days, is it?"

"I see nothing wrong with continuing on as we have," Ethel said firmly. "We still have Pastor Ley, and he suits me just fine."

The three sisters exchanged surprised looks.

Alice had known and worked with Henry Ley at church for years, and knew he was a kind and gentle man who had made many friends throughout the community. The problem was, Henry was afflicted with a speech impediment that caused him to stammer whenever he tried to speak more than a few words at a time. When he became nervous, the stammering grew worse—and what made Henry more nervous than anything else was public speaking.

Despite his handicap, Henry had tried valiantly in his position as assistant pastor to fill in for Daniel Howard after his death. Listening and watching him struggle through a sermon was an ordeal for everyone, however, and always wrenched at Alice's heart.

"I like Henry, too, but we can't pretend that he could ever replace our father." Louise turned to Alice. "Nevertheless, you have already offered him the position of head pastor, have you not?"

"Several times," Alice said, "and he's refused. Henry does know his limitations better than anyone, and he really doesn't want the job."

Ethel waved her hand in a dismissive gesture. "So Henry has a little problem speaking—"

"A *little* problem?" Jane's brows rose. "Auntie, Henry can barely get through a full sentence without tripping all over it. Everyone ends up trying to finish them for him."

"Henry and Patsy Ley have lived in Acorn Hill most of their lives," her aunt snapped. "They're a part of our community. Your father wouldn't want some outsider coming in to take over for him. He loved the people of this town, and always wanted the best for them."

"I think your loyalty to Father is admirable, Aunt Ethel,

but we have to be realistic." Louise dropped a cube of sugar into her tea and stirred it. "Public speaking is an ordeal for Henry, and obviously we cannot go on with these guest ministers." She rubbed her temple. "As it is, I feel like I'm attending open auditions every week instead of worship."

"A new minister is exactly what this town needs," Jane stated. "Someone young, maybe from Philadelphia or another city. He'd be able to provide a more modern ministry—and Lord knows, this town could certainly use that."

"Actually, congregations in most large cities tend to be long established and very traditional," Alice said, "so there is no guarantee that a minister from the city will have a more modern view on things."

"There's nothing wrong with tradition, Jane. We like Acorn Hill and Grace Chapel just the way they are," Ethel insisted, then turned to Alice. "You feel the same, don't you, dear?"

Since she served on the church board with her aunt, Alice had equal responsibility in selecting her father's replacement. She could not agree with her aunt, however—the parish needed a new minister for many reasons, and not just to give sermons on Sunday.

Daniel Howard had been the spiritual center for the people of Acorn Hill, and his death had left a terrible gap in the community. Mutual grief over his passing had drawn everyone together at first, but now that the pain was easing, only the empty space remained. Alice knew the congregation was beginning to drift apart, with some people going to other churches and others descending into apathy. They needed someone to guide them, to inspire them, to fill that space in their lives.

"With Father gone, nothing will ever be the same again," Alice said. The familiar pangs of grief over Daniel's death made her heart constrict. "I don't want to see things change either, Aunt Ethel, but we have to think of the needs of the people who belong to our church."

Louise gave her a sharp look. "Surely by now the board has *someone* in mind."

Alice saw Jane look down into her tea. She wished she could discuss the problems the board was having with Louise, who was very good at sorting out such difficulties, but it would probably be wiser to wait until their aunt was not part of the conversation.

"We have a board meeting tomorrow morning," Ethel said. "But we haven't agreed on anyone who has applied so far."

And we may not, Alice suspected, *if Aunt Ethel doesn't stop opposing every minister we interview.*

Because Grace Chapel Inn was a bed and breakfast, the three Howard sisters had to get an early start every day. None of them minded it in the least. As a nurse, Alice was used to odd hours. Jane's work as a chef had trained her to rise at dawn. Louise herself had never liked sleeping in late, and found herself incapable of doing so since the death of her husband. Since opening the inn, the sisters had worked out their duties so that they spent the first half hour together in the kitchen, before Jane needed to begin preparing breakfast for the guests. It was a comfortable time when they could share coffee or tea and the morning paper, and talk over their plans for the day.

"Kenneth Thompson spoke to me last night," Louise said as she brought a basket of Jane's flaky croissants to the table. "The sink in his bathroom is dripping again."

"I'll call Fred and ask him to stop in and see if the tap needs to be replaced." Alice opened the morning paper and took out the lifestyle section, then passed the rest to her older sister. "Is there anything else I should ask Fred to take a look at?"

"Not that I can think of. Oh, Rev. Thompson also requested a clock radio with a different alarm. Evidently he tested the one in his room and it's too loud." Louise sat down and fastened the chain holding her reading glasses around her neck. "Do we have an extra one?"

"I'll swap his with the one in my room," Jane offered. "Mine has an adjustable volume on it."

Alice selected one of the crescent-shaped French pastries for herself, trying not to disturb the flaky golden crust as she did so. "How many students do you have this afternoon, Louise?"

"Only one, Sissy Matthews." Louise, who had been taking piano students part-time to supplement their income, smiled. "She's doing very well, but then she has a natural ear for music."

"Does she really?" Jane looked skeptical. "I heard her playing the other day, and it sounded like she was using a hammer on the keys."

Louise sighed. "No, that was her brother Charles. He thinks the harder he bangs on them, the better he plays."

"Well, if anyone can stop him from ending up a heavy-handed piano-wrecker, it's you, Louise," Jane said. "After all, you did teach me to play 'Heart and Soul.'"

Louise gave her youngest sister a dry look. "Thank you for the vote of confidence."

Jane's lack of musical ability was something of an inside family joke. She could sing, but was always slightly off-key, and had been hopeless with any musical instrument. Years before, Louise had tried to help her sister with her piano lessons, but had only succeeded in teaching her how to play one song, and only then after weeks and weeks of patient instruction. Later a music teacher in school tested Jane and revealed that she was completely tone-deaf.

"I'm off duty at the hospital until tomorrow, so I'll man the desk once I get back from the board meeting." Alice thought for a moment. "Rev. Highland is checking out today, I think, and the Goldings will be arriving on Friday."

"They're the ones bringing their children with them,

aren't they?" Jane brought the coffee pot over to the table and refilled her sisters' mugs. "Will they have enough room?"

"They decided at the last minute to leave their oldest son and daughter at home with their grandparents, so there will only be three kids instead of five. It will be tight, but Mrs. Golding said they're bringing their own portable crib for the baby and sleeping bags for the other two." Alice smiled. "It will be nice to have children in the house again."

"We better go up and child-proof their room before they arrive," Louise decided with her usual practicality. "I put the outlet covers and the baby monitor in the second floor storage closet." She put on her reading glasses and opened the front page of the business section. "Jane, would you make a pot of decaf? Rev. Thompson mentioned that is all he drinks."

"I've already started brewing it." Jane sat down and removed the cooking section from the paper. "I thought I'd make some chocolate-cherry scones for tea this afternoon. Do you think Kenneth and the other guests would enjoy those?"

Her casual use of the minister's first name made Louise and Alice exchange a glance, but before either could comment, there was a knock and the kitchen door opened.

Jane put down her paper and smiled. "Speak of the pastor."

"Good morning." Kenneth had exchanged his conservative suit for a pair of dark navy trousers and a lightweight blue sweater over a white dress shirt. "I thought I'd get an early start today, but I couldn't resist the smell of coffee." He glanced around the table. "I'm not intruding on family time, am I?"

"Not at all." Jane rose from her chair. "Do you take cream, sugar, both?"

"Black will be fine, thank you." He checked his watch, then looked up and frowned. "Is that the correct time?" He nodded toward the wall clock over the table.

"No, it's fast. We keep all the clocks in the inn set ahead

five minutes," Alice admitted. When he gave her an odd look, she added, "When I'm in a hurry, I forget that they're set ahead. It helps me be on time versus five minutes late for everything. It's sort of a family habit."

"I see." Kenneth didn't sound as if he approved. "Would any of you ladies know where I can purchase a map of the local area?"

Louise grew thoughtful as she considered his question. "I don't think Nine Lives Bookstore carries any, but there may be some regional and state maps at the drugstore or the gas station."

"I've already purchased those." His dark brows drew together as he took out his notebook and scanned the first page. "I was hoping to find one for Acorn Hill, Potterston and the surrounding townships."

Jane chuckled as she brought his coffee to him. "This town is so small, Pastor, I think I could draw a map of it on a cocktail napkin."

"I appreciate the thought, but I think I will stop in town and see what I can find." He set the notebook aside before taking the cup from Jane. "I have a number of things to do on my schedule for the day, and getting lost isn't one of them."

"If you do, just ask someone for directions," Louise told him. "People here are very friendly, and they'll be happy to help you."

"That I have noticed." He sampled the dark brew, then smiled. "This is really excellent, Jane."

"I can't abide decaf that tastes like dishwater." Jane opened the door to the dining room. "Come and sit down, and I'll show you our breakfast menu."

After Jane and Kenneth had left, Alice folded her section of the newspaper. "He seems like a nice, likeable man. Very detail oriented."

"Rather fussy, if you ask me." Louise skillfully added

some orange marmalade to her croissant. "Always making notes and wanting things just so. And who makes out a 'schedule for the day,' I ask you?"

"Well, you . . . that is, *we* do." Alice laughed at her sister's indignant expression. "We simply don't write ours down in a little notebook."

With all the candidates coming to town to interview for the position of pastor, the church board had been meeting twice a week in the Grace Chapel Assembly Room. They had been searching for more than a month and still couldn't agree on the right man to hire for the job.

Because she was accustomed to taking notes for doctors on rounds at the hospital, Alice had volunteered to act as board secretary, and she opened the meeting by reading the minutes from their last session.

"The board voted five to four against hiring candidate Eugene Smith as head pastor for Grace Chapel," Alice read from her neatly written notes. "Mayor Tynan and Ms. Simpson stated that they felt Rev. Smith did not have enough prior experience for the position, while Mr. Overstreet and Mrs. Songer felt his credentials were more than adequate."

"Which they were," Sylvia Songer responded, sounding slightly annoyed. The seamstress and owner of Sylvia's Buttons was one of Acorn Hill's busiest shopkeepers, and her dark eyes and quick gestures often made Alice think of a little brown sparrow. Sylvia had enjoyed Rev. Smith's guest sermon, at which he asked the congregation to stand and join hands as he played the guitar and sang his own enthusiastic version of "The Old Rugged Cross." "Isn't that really the issue here? We want someone with the right qualifications."

"Sylvia, I have shoes that are older than Rev. Smith," Florence Simpson said as she adjusted one of her frilly sleeves. Aside from Ethel, the plump, rather prissy woman was the board member most resistant to change. "Do remember that half of our congregation are over the age of forty. They're not going to be comfortable with such a young minister."

Cyril Overstreet, a quiet, older man with a dry sense of humor, glanced under the table. "Your shoes don't look all that old, Florence."

"This is age discrimination," Sylvia insisted.

"No, it's common sense," Ethel said, siding with Florence as she generally did. "Land sakes, I can't see myself confiding my troubles to a minister young enough to be my grandson!"

"Well, I could," June Carter said. As owner of the Coffee Shop, she felt at ease talking to everyone and anyone.

"Hold on, now," Fred Humbert said. The town philosopher and an amateur weather prognosticator, Fred owned his own hardware store and took care of most of the carpentry and handyman work around town. As head of the church board, it was his responsibility to keep their discussions orderly. "I liked Pastor Smith too, but I agree with Florence and Ethel. He needs a bit more time behind the pulpit before he can take on a job like this."

"And that guitar business—absolutely disgraceful," Ethel murmured to Florence. "Singing hymns like they were pop music." She shook her head.

Cyril overheard her remark and leaned forward to catch her gaze. "I play pop music for my indoor plants, Mrs. Buckley, and you know something? They grow like weeds."

Ethel snorted. "More likely they're trying to escape from all that racket."

Alice took advantage of the pause and continued reading. "The board then conducted the interview with Rev. Winchell."

"The movie star minister," Mayor Lloyd Tynan muttered as he loosened his bow tie.

"Jealous, Mayor?" Sylvia's eyes were bright with amusement. "I don't think he'd work in a town that doesn't have a TV or radio station."

It was Florence's turn to be indignant. "He gave a fine sermon! 'Telling It on the Mountain' was an excellent theme."

"He certainly rehearsed it enough times." Lloyd rolled his eyes. "Ethel and I saw him in the parlor at Grace Chapel Inn while he was staying there, telling it to the sofa."

"I don't know about the rest of you, but I certainly preferred him to that Rev. Highland." Sylvia suppressed a shudder. "My goodness, he was a stern one. All that finger-wagging he did at the congregation."

Now Lloyd sat up. "Rev. Highland believes in tradition and being a strong authority figure, and there's nothing wrong with that."

"Maybe we should consider hiring an interim minister," Fred suggested. "I was reading an article about a fella who travels around and works exclusively with churches undergoing major changes. He stays long enough to bring things back to a healthy status, then leaves when a permanent minister can be hired."

"You mean, we'd have to go through this *two* times?" Sylvia groaned and propped her head against one hand. "I'm already getting behind on orders at the shop as it is."

Fred cleared his throat. "Folks, why don't we let Alice finish reading the minutes before we get down to new business?"

"Those are really all the notes that I have," Alice said quickly. "The board scheduled to reconvene today to discuss the candidate issue again. We said a prayer of thanks, and the meeting was adjourned." She closed her notebook and sat down.

"Discuss the candidate issue?" June sat back, amused. "Gee, I thought we were just going to start bickering with each other like we did at the last meeting."

"June." Alice gave her a beseeching look. "Please."

"W-w-we have to choose s-someone," associate Pastor Henry Ley put in. As always, the sound of his own faltering voice made him tense, and he had to try two times to get the last word out. "S-s-soon."

"Why can't we go on as we have?" Ethel wanted to know, just as she had back at Grace Chapel Inn. "Henry is a fine minister." Before he could respond, she added quickly, "Now I know you're a bit shy about speaking, Henry, but Daniel never minded, and neither do we."

"I m-m-mind, Ethel." Henry flushed, but doggedly continued forcing the words from his mouth. "I'm f-f-flattered, of c-c-course, but I c-c-can't accept. T-this is n-n-not a j-job for m-me."

Ethel folded her arms. "You're the one person who Daniel would have wanted to succeed him as head minister, Henry."

"How do you know that, Mrs. Buckley?" Sylvia asked. "Maybe Pastor Howard wanted someone else. He's not here for us to ask, so we'll never know."

"I know, Sylvia Songer." Alice's aunt grew indignant. "I know because Daniel was my *brother*."

"I don't think Father ever expected Pastor Ley to take the job as head minister, Aunt Ethel," Alice felt she had to say. She turned immediately to reassure the associate pastor. "You know he was very fond of you, Henry, but he also knew how difficult it was for you to speak in public."

Indeed, her father had always been rather protective of Henry. Even after Daniel retired, he continued to give the sermons on Sundays to spare Pastor Ley the ordeal of public speaking. He would not have approved of Ethel's pressuring Henry to take on the position at all, but her aunt stubbornly refused to see it that way, as she proved with the next thing she said.

"We're not trying to force you, Henry," Ethel said in a cajoling way. "It's just you know the church and the congregation as well as Daniel did."

"Pastor Ley has said no twice now, Ethel," Fred pointed out. "We shouldn't badger him about his decision."

Alice made a new notation on her pad and cautiously suggested, "Maybe we should move on to new business and discuss the next candidates?"

"Here are the latest resumés." Lloyd passed out copies to each member of the board. "Rev. Bruce Golding from Charlotte, North Carolina, and Rev. Kenneth Thompson from Boston, Massachusetts. I suggest we review them now, as Rev. Thompson will be coming in today for his interview, and Rev. Golding on Friday."

Florence Simpson had a habit of reading under her breath, then making odd comments out loud to herself as she went along. "Never heard of that college. Misspelled that word." She sat back in her chair, then peered at the resumé again. "Land sakes, *how* many children?"

Alice saw her aunt only skim quickly through both men's resumés before she placed them back in the folder. She couldn't have read them, but then, Ethel had gotten that stubborn look in her eye again. Alice had a terrible feeling that her aunt had already made up her mind to have Henry Ley or no one at all.

Father would know how to bring her around, she thought as she brooded over what to do. *It's times like these that I really miss him the most.*

Both men's resumés were impressive. Bruce Golding had sent in several excellent letters of reference and had served as an associate, then head minister for eight years at his previous parish. He had a strong background in youth ministry and family counseling, and listed his personal interests as outdoor sports and gardening.

Kenneth Thompson had approximately the same amount of experience, with the additional benefit of an excellent education. He had also devoted a great deal of time to missions providing relief for the poor, elderly and sick in the metropolitan Boston area. His personal interests included woodworking and furniture restoration.

Alice tried to imagine the precise, tidy man she had met yesterday serving meals to homeless people and conducting Sunday services for patients at hospital chapels. His appearance suggested someone more suited to being a businessman or a doctor than a minister. He was also from the city, where life moved much faster than it did in Acorn Hill.

Truth be told, she was not very enthusiastic about the thought of Rev. Thompson's serving as head minister. He seemed so out of place, and although he was polite, he didn't seem like a very warm person at all.

"Remember what God told Samuel, Alice," her father had once said when she had mentioned being afraid of a new, stern-looking teacher at school. "'The Lord does not look at the things man looks at. Man looks at the outward appearance, but the Lord looks at the heart.'" Daniel had been right, too. The particular teacher had turned out to be a gentle, dedicated woman who never spoke a cross word to any of her students. Alice had ended up liking her more than any other teacher she would ever have.

But does that mean Kenneth Thompson is the right minister for us? Try as she might, Alice could not imagine him taking her father's place at Grace Chapel. *What if he's not, and we don't find out until it's too late?*

Fred Humbert, responding to the sound of knocking, opened the door to the Assembly Room, and then turned to announce, "Rev. Kenneth Thompson is here, folks."

Chapter ⛪ Three

All the board members had their questions prepared for Rev. Thompson. Everyone took a moment to inspect the visiting minister, who was wearing a finely tailored dark gray suit, before Fred briefly introduced himself and each member of the board.

"We appreciate you taking the time to meet with us today, Pastor Thompson," the mayor said after everyone had offered greetings. "Have you been finding your way around town all right?"

"Yes, I have, thank you. Everyone has been very helpful," Kenneth said.

"That's always good to hear." Lloyd was pleased. "We folks in Acorn Hill pride ourselves on being friendly."

Alice glanced at the serious faces around her and wished the same could be said of the church board.

"We should get started now." Fred opened his folder. "The purpose of asking you to this interview is to give the members of the church board an opportunity to learn more about you and your call to ministry. You've already filled out the background and service questionnaires, so all we'd like to do is ask you some questions now."

Sylvia Songer took advantage of Fred's pause to add,

"With your education and certifications, you've more than met our minimum guidelines for the position." She gave Florence a direct look. "Just so you're aware of that, Pastor."

"Yes, well." Fred cleared his throat. "We'll move right along to questions from our individual board members. Sylvia, since you're so on the ball today, why don't you go first?"

"I'd be happy to," the seamstress said. "Pastor Thompson, in what way has your call to ministry been most challenged since you dedicated yourself to a life of service?"

Alice cringed a little. Sylvia was enthusiastic but she also asked some of the toughest questions.

"I would have to say losing my wife Catherine was the greatest personal challenge I've faced to date," Kenneth said, very calmly. "It was my wife's work that originally inspired me to become a minister, and I admit that I had always envisioned her at my side. I know I will continue to face that challenge every day for the rest of my life."

Sylvia thanked him and sat back as June Carter took her turn. "Pastor Thompson, how have you best served Christ in the church, and what have you learned about yourself from your ministry?" Her lips curved in a smile as she added, "Mine's a two-parter."

Kenneth smiled back and nodded. "I believe I've best served Christ by not limiting myself to a single ministry. In working with the poor and the homeless, I've brought the Word to people who needed to hear it. But that's no more important than bringing it to the pulpit every Sunday, because the congregation in church needs to hear it just as much." He leaned forward, using his hands to make an encompassing gesture as he spoke. "What I've learned about myself I can't adequately express with a definitive answer. The different ministries in which I've been involved have taught me there are an infinite number of ways to serve Christ and bring others closer to God, and the people with whom I've worked have inspired me day after day. Maybe the most important thing I've learned about myself is that I will always be learning."

The questions continued. Lloyd asked the minister to describe his spiritual mentors, and Florence asked a rather pointed question about what gifts for ministry Kenneth felt he did not have. Alice could barely keep from chuckling when Kenneth confessed that, like her sister Jane, he was not at all musically gifted.

"Our choir director actually requested that I not try to accompany the congregation during our hymns," he admitted. "Evidently I was drowning out the first row sopranos."

Then it was Fred's turn. "I'd like to know what made you decide to interview for this position, Pastor. Acorn Hill is a far cry from a big city like Boston."

"It's true that I've never lived in a small town, but I spent some of my happiest childhood times in one. When I was a boy, my parents allowed me to visit my grandfather every summer. He lived in a small fishing village where life was peaceful and quiet and yet very rewarding. All the people regarded others to be their neighbors, no matter where they lived in the village, and they took the time to enjoy life." He glanced out the window at the antique shop across the road. "My grandfather's village is a tourist attraction now, and most of the people who lived there when I was a youngster have moved away, but over the years I've longed to find another place like it. When I learned of the opportunity here in Acorn Hill, it seemed exactly what I've been looking for."

Finally, it was time for the last question, which was Alice's.

It was not so much a question as it was an invitation to talk about his work, which Alice preferred. "Pastor Thompson, tell us about someone you have led to Christ recently."

He seemed surprised by that, then thought for a moment before he spoke. "I was visiting a very poor neighborhood on the west side of Boston a few months ago as part of a project to bring meals to the elderly and to shut-ins. In one building, the elevator was out of order, and we had to carry the food up six flights of stairs. An old lady in a sixth-floor apartment had a bad hip, and could no longer stand the pain of walking up and down all those stairs. She told me that although her landlord could well afford to make the repairs, he refused to fix the elevator."

Alice noticed Fred frowning. As the town handyman, he couldn't understand anyone's leaving something fixable in disrepair. Neither could Alice, especially as the man had the money to address the problem.

"I went to see the landlord myself the next day, hoping I could convince him to do something about the situation. He was a wealthy real estate agent who had done very well for himself and had a fine office in a beautiful building downtown. I told him about the problem, and the tenant, and he promised me that he would look into it." Kenneth smiled sadly. "The next week I went to the building again on my rounds and found that the elevator was still out of order. After I delivered the food to the lady on the sixth floor, I went over to speak to the landlord again."

"I'd have given him a piece of my mind," Sylvia muttered under her breath.

Alice thought of the poor old woman—she must have felt like a prisoner in her own apartment. "What happened, Pastor Thompson?" she couldn't help asking.

"The landlord wasn't quite as polite as he had been the week before. He told me he would have the elevator repaired when he had time to get around to it. I told him that was not what God wanted him to do. He laughed and said that he didn't believe in God." Kenneth folded his arms. "So I made a bet with him."

"You made a bet?" Florence sounded shocked.

"Yes, ma'am, I did. I bet the landlord that if he came to

my church for services every Sunday for a month, that by the last Sunday he would not only believe in God, but he would start doing God's work. The terms of the bet were that if I was right, he would fix the elevator immediately. If I was wrong, I would pay to repair the elevator myself."

"I wouldn't want those odds," Cyril murmured.

"That Sunday, the landlord came to my church, and my ushers brought him up to the very front row. That's where all the tenants from his building and other people from the same neighborhood were seated. The lady from the sixth floor sat next to him, with her wheelchair in the aisle." He smiled at the stunned faces of the board members. "Before I began services, I took a moment and introduced him to his tenants. You see, he had never actually met any of them."

All on the board seemed to be holding their breath. Finally Sylvia said, "I bet he was really uncomfortable. Those people must have hated him."

"No, they didn't hate him," Kenneth replied. "They worshipped God with the landlord in their midst and offered him their fellowship. They never said an unkind word to the man. I believe they pitied him."

They're better people than I am, Alice thought. *I'd have given him a good talking to.*

"For the next three Sundays after that, the landlord came to our Sunday service. He waited for someone to lash out at him, but he was treated with nothing but respect and kindness—the very things that he had denied the people who lived in his building. All the landlord had to do was sit through each service and listen to others praying for God to help them with whatever troubles they were having. Naturally many of those troubles were his fault."

"Ah." Lloyd nodded his approval.

"Week by week, the influence of prayer and Scripture had an increasingly profound effect on him. At the end of the fourth service, the landlord waited in the church until everyone else had left, and then he came up to me and told me that he would fix the elevator. He asked me what else he could do to help the people who lived in his building."

Alice let out a breath she hadn't known she was holding. "It worked."

Ethel gave him a narrow look. "All that, just to bring one man to Christ?"

"Not exactly, ma'am. You see, I actually made two bets. One with the landlord, and one with the people in his building and their neighbors. I promised them that if they came to church for a month, and truly tried to forgive the landlord for his neglect, that either he or I would repair the elevator."

No one said anything, but Lloyd coughed suddenly into his handkerchief, and Fred seemed to be studying the ceiling intently.

"The landlord is still a very wealthy man in material terms, with a fine office in a beautiful building downtown, but he is far richer now than he ever was before, as a result of receiving the gift of faith. Every Saturday now, he supervises bringing meals to elderly and infirm people in the poor neighborhoods of Boston—he took over my old job, in fact. Every Sunday, he volunteers to drive those people without transportation to church. As for his own building, he's renovating it to make it a better place for his tenants to live." He paused for a moment. "And the elevator works just fine now."

After finishing up the last of her tasks in the kitchen, Jane came into the office to see if Louise needed her help. Her sister was recording expenses in one of her ledgers, and had several neat stacks of receipts piled around her on the desk. Wendell sat on one side of the desk and watched the movements of her pen as she wrote the figures in each column.

"No, dear, I am nearly finished with this."

"How are we doing?" Jane nodded toward the ledger.

"Very well. We have managed to keep expenses under control, and with all the reservations, we'll turn a nice profit this month. Wendell, stop that." Louise frowned as the tabby gave her pen a gentle swat with his paw.

Jane reached over and scratched the back of the cat's head. "If you don't need me for anything, I was thinking of walking into town."

Her sister looked over the rim of her reading glasses at the wall clock. "Alice will be home soon from the church board meeting, and I can cover the front desk and the phone until then. What do you need in town?"

"I wanted to stop by Nine Lives and see if Viola had any books on how to get rid of certain sneaky, slimy garden pests." She saw Wendell eyeing a pile of receipts and scooped him up in her arms. "Since someone furry, who shall remain nameless, hasn't been hunting them down for me." She rubbed the tip of her nose against Wendell's.

The tabby gave a light sneeze and shook his head, then jumped down to the floor. He sauntered out of the office to investigate a patch of sunshine by one of the front windows.

"Go right ahead." Louise shooed her toward the door with one hand.

Jane stopped in the foyer to get her straw hat from the bentwood rack, then started down the drive. The walk from the inn to the center of Acorn Hill was a pleasant one, and the afternoon sunshine felt good on her shoulders. *What a lovely day,* Jane thought. Wildflowers on the side of Chapel Road bobbed their heads as if in agreement.

Most of Acorn Hill's shops lined both sides of Hill Street, which intersected with Chapel Road between Fred's Hardware and the Coffee Shop. People strolled leisurely down sidewalks on either side of the two-lane road, looking in at the always-interesting displays of vintage glassware and clothing at Acorn Hill Antiques, or the mouth-watering trays of buns, muffins and cookies at the Good Apple Bakery.

Across the street, tidy racks of indoor and outdoor plants sat outside Craig Tracy's Wild Things garden shop, and Jane spotted a particularly gorgeous feathery fern in the window. Craig, who was a relative newcomer to Acorn Hill, had the magic touch with plants, and she often stopped in to chat with him. He had already discussed the slug problem in her garden with her, but she was reluctant to resort to the pesticide he had recommended.

"There has to be a way to live and let live," she'd told him. "I don't want to kill them; I just want them to dine— somewhere else."

He had laughed at that. "You're far too softhearted for a gardener, Ms. Howard. It's survival of the fittest."

Viola Reed's Nine Lives Bookstore sat at the corner of Berry Lane and Chapel Road, across the road from the General Store. It was a small building with white walls and a cheerful red roof, and a beveled glass door with the names of the shop and the proprietor scrolled in fine gold letters. A wrought iron bench sat beside the front door, and patrons would often find Viola sitting there with two or three of her cats, reading while her felines basked in the sunshine.

Today Viola was changing the books on the shelves in her window display, replacing the current selection with a set of Mark Twain novels with handsome, dark green bindings. The proprietor of the bookshop was somewhat eccentric—she always wore large, colorful scarves tied dramatically about her throat and shoulders—and always assertive with her opinions. She was very good friends with Louise, too, which Jane thought owed as much to mutual respect as their shared love of classic literature.

When she saw Jane approaching, Viola set aside the books she was holding and came to meet her at the door. "Good afternoon, Jane. I haven't seen you in ages, come in. Watch out for Byron there." She nodded toward a pile of black fur on the floor mat just inside the door.

"Hello, Viola." Jane carefully stepped over one of Viola's many cats, an old fellow who was sprawled on his back and sleeping peacefully. The Nine Lives bookshop was redolent of old leather and books, a scent Jane found very appealing, as it reminded her of her father's study. "How have you been?"

"I can't complain." The bookshop owner straightened her golden scarf, which had been designed to look like an old world map, complete with lettering in Latin. "What brings you to my corner of town?"

"I'm looking for a gardening book." Jane briefly described the problem with the slugs, then added, "I'd like something that uses an organic method, something that won't kill them but will chase them away from my plants."

"*Hmm.*" Viola thought for a moment. "I don't carry a big selection of garden books, but let me look through what I have. They're back this way."

Jane followed the older woman to a corner of the shop, where she had a number of books on plants and herbs displayed on one shelf. Beside them, oddly enough, was a rack of best-selling legal thrillers.

"I didn't expect Grisham alongside gardening," Jane said, eyeing the titles.

"*Pffft.*" Viola waved a hand at the paperbacks. "I only carry those for people who can't appreciate fine literature. And that describes far too many people in this town, if you ask me. By the way," she looked over her bifocals, "when was the last time you read a good book?"

"Do romance novels count?"

"Absolutely not." Viola removed a heavy volume from a top shelf and checked the table of contents.

"Then probably not since the seventh grade." Jane grinned, then noticed an old book sitting on top of a carton by the back door. It had an eye-catching red and white cover, with a lovely sketch of a quaint farmhouse and barn.

"I'm running a special on Mark Twain this week," Viola

told her. "You'd really enjoy *A Connecticut Yankee in King Arthur's Court*."

"What's this?" Jane went over and picked up the red and white book, which bore the title *A Treasury of Pennsylvania Dutch Cooking*.

"That's an old cookbook I picked up in a secondhand shop over in Lancaster." Viola replaced the gardening book and joined her. "Probably from the thirties or forties, from the look of it. I was going to use it for my Summer Festival display."

Jane opened the cover and skimmed the pages, noting a remarkable range of unusual recipes. Some appeared to be in German, but most were in English. "Oh, this is wonderful, Viola. Look, there's a whole section here on aspics."

"Meat jellies?" The older woman shuddered. "I never understood why people liked those."

"They're very nutritious, and perfect during the summer instead of hot entrees." She flipped through the section. "There are recipes here for *boova shenkel*, rabbit cake, and something called *fastnachts*." The exotic names intrigued her.

"My grandmother used to make *fastnachts*, but she called them Dutch festival doughnuts. She was raised in Lancaster County, you know, and grew up with the Amish. She'd bring over a big batch of them every year on Shrove Tuesday, with a big jug of molasses."

Jane smiled as she read some homey advice at the end of a dessert recipe. "Listen to this: 'A good cake for company, but cut in thin slices, very rich.'" Jane continued to browse through her discovery. "I wonder why anyone would let go of such a treasure."

"Those are the words of a veteran cook. If you like it that much, Jane, why don't you take it? I was only going to have it as a decoration; you'd probably get much more use out of it. Maybe you can find some recipes in there for your guests at the inn."

"Me, cook Pennsylvania Dutch style?" Jane chuckled at the notion, then grew serious. "You know, it's not a bad idea. I've been meaning to try out some regional dishes, and these look like the real thing."

Viola smiled. "Well, if I can't sell you on Mark Twain, at least I'll have you reading one classic."

That Sunday Jane asked Alice to help her in the kitchen while Louise served their guests. With all the rooms at the inn filled and the Goldings' room holding five, Jane had fourteen meals to prepare. Some of the guests had special dietary requirements, and a folding table had to be put in place for the Goldings, at their request.

"This egg-white omelet is for Mrs. Golding," Jane told Alice as she handed her the plate for the finishing prep. "And the vegetarian quiche is for Mrs. Alcott. She also gets the grapefruit instead of the orange slices. We'll have to hurry with clearing up if we don't want to be late for services."

"Goodness, Jane, we have at least two hours before church starts." She frowned at her sister's bare wrist. "Why aren't you wearing your watch?"

"I think I dropped it somewhere." Jane began scooping cinnamon-apple oatmeal from a warming pot into bowls for the younger Goldings. "I'm looking forward to hearing Rev. Thompson speak, aren't you?"

Alice added fresh fruit and sprigs of mint as garnishes to each plate. "Actually, Rev. Thompson checked out this morning, but he'll be back next weekend. Rev. Golding will be giving the sermon, and then he and his family will be leaving earlier than they planned—his wife isn't feeling well." She placed the finished plates on a tray and carried them to the door in time to meet Louise coming in from the dining room. "Everything all right?"

"We need another pitcher of orange juice for the Goldings'

table." Louise looked faintly harassed and there were some small orange splash marks on her apron. "And please tell me that the oatmeal is ready—the children are getting very boisterous." She swiped at her apron with a paper towel.

Jane quickly topped the bowls of oatmeal with finely diced apples, nutmeg and a sprinkle of powdered sugar. "Ready to go. Alice and I will bring them in, Louise. You put on the tea kettle and take a break for a few minutes."

As she carried the tray out to the Goldings' table, Jane couldn't help smiling. The couple's three children were all lively, tow-headed youngsters with boundless energy, and they kept everyone on their toes from the moment they got up until their extremely patient mother settled them in for the night.

Joyce Golding, a small, sturdy woman of seemingly infinite fortitude, gave her a grateful smile as Jane placed extra napkins on the table and helped her to distribute the bowls. "Thank you, Ms. Howard. Eating out with the children is always something of a challenge."

Jane mopped up a stray splash of orange juice. "I don't know how you do it, Mrs. Golding."

"Joyce keeps threatening to run off to the circus to become a trapeze artist," Rev. Golding said, winking at his wife. "But I tell her that she'd be bored to tears in a week."

"Oh, I don't know." His wife looked thoughtful. "I could probably do some lion taming on the side, in my spare time."

"I like the circus." The oldest boy, who was five, wrinkled his nose at the bowl. "But I don't want oatmeal. I want frosted cereal."

His younger sister, who clearly worshipped her brother, immediately chimed in, "So do I!"

The baby of the family, an energetic toddler, began banging her spoon on the tray of her high chair and screeching nonsense words as if in agreement with her siblings.

Their mother, who Jane thought was looking a little tired and washed out, sighed. "Children, please, eat your breakfast. We don't want to be late for church—your father is giving the sermon today."

"But Mom, we want frosted cereal," her son wailed.

"Oh, dear. We're fresh out of frosted cereal," Alice said, and reached to remove their bowls. "Jane, you have some liver and onions left, don't you?"

"Sure, I made a double batch this morning," Jane said, playing along. "I'll just go and get some for the kids."

"Liver?" The girl's face scrunched up and she clamped her hands around her bowl. "That's yucky!"

"*Hmm*. Well, if you don't want the liver and onions, I think there's some creamed spinach left over from dinner last night," Alice said.

"And some pickled beets," Jane added for good measure.

The little boy's eyes rounded, and then he gulped. "I like oatmeal better."

"Me, too," his sister said, and put a big spoonful in her mouth.

"I'll have to remember that one," their father said, winking at Jane.

She suppressed a chuckle and went to help Alice refill coffee cups and clear away the finished plates from the main table.

"I can't believe Father's old liver, spinach and beets trick still works," she told Alice on the way back into the kitchen. "Good thinking."

"I wish I could use it on the church board," Alice said ruefully. "Unfortunately, the prospect of pickled beets probably wouldn't intimidate them very much."

Louise handed them each a cup of tea. "Are they *still* debating over whom to hire?"

"We've never stopped." Alice sat down for a moment. "We've gone over the list of candidates and their resumes a hundred times, but it's like serving on a hung jury—there is no agreement on anything or anyone."

"Well, someone has to make a decision." Jane loaded the

dishwasher and then wiped her hands on a towel. "I think Kenneth would be perfect for the job, especially after you told me that story about how he brought that greedy landlord over to God."

"Don't forget all his tenants, too. He is very qualified, and his interview was excellent." Alice glanced at the door to the dining room. "But Rev. Golding did very well, too."

Jane sat down and rested her chin against her fist. "So who do you think will get the job?"

Alice looked uncomfortable. "To be honest, I think it will be Rev. Golding. He's a little more approachable than Rev. Thompson. I think the board felt Kenneth was, well, a little too self-assured."

"That's a problem?" Jane's brows rose.

"Acorn Hill is not like Boston, Jane," Louise reminded her. "He might be better suited to a congregation in the city."

"A couple of the board members felt he lacked warmth," Alice said. "He's never worked in a small town, the way Rev. Golding has. He also doesn't have the same sense of humor."

"That's ridiculous." Jane felt cross; she liked Kenneth Thompson more than any other candidate who had come to Acorn Hill. "Having confidence in yourself isn't a crime, you know. It certainly has nothing to do with how well you relate to others. Nor does where you've lived. And he has a fine sense of humor. It's just . . . subtle, is all."

"Oh, I agree with you," Alice hastily assured her. "It's just that some of the board members aren't sure the congregation will accept him. He's not like Father at all."

"No one will ever be like our father was, and they should realize that," Louise stated. "This debate has gone on too long, Alice. A decision has to be made."

Jane thought so, too, but their middle sister had always gravitated toward being more of a peacemaker than a debater. Which meant Alice wouldn't rock the boat, and Kenneth Thompson was probably out of luck.

Chapter ✤ Four

Louise felt tired and slightly cranky as she took her seat in church. She usually enjoyed the hour of prayer and fellowship at Grace Chapel, but the many guest ministers giving sermons on Sunday made her feel unsettled. So did the church board's inability to make a decision.

The Howard sisters always sat together, along with their Aunt Ethel and Lloyd Tynan. Louise had been unable to find her Bible that morning, so Ethel sat beside her to share hers.

"Did you leave it somewhere?" her aunt asked.

"Probably." That was the other reason she felt so at odds with everything. Louise had never been an absent-minded person, but lately she had lost track of several items. The Bible was the latest, and it was one she particularly treasured. Eliot had given it to her when they were married, and she had written Cynthia's date of birth in it. Over the years her husband had read from it to their daughter, and later it always seemed to fall open to one of his favorite verses. She had even written the date of his death in it, along with the prayer she had read at his funeral.

Maybe this is a sign, Louise thought. *I'm just getting old and forgetful.* That made her feel even more depressed. How could she keep up with her two younger sisters and the business at the inn if she couldn't remember where she put things?

Ethel suddenly frowned—Kenneth Thompson had stopped by their pew.

Louise was surprised to see him—she had assumed that he had checked out of the inn to get an early start on his trip back to Boston.

The visiting minister gestured to the empty space beside Jane. "Would you mind if I sit with you and your family for services?"

"Please do." Jane immediately moved over, making more space for him.

Louise felt her aunt's disapproval but allowed herself to smile at Kenneth. He looked very attractive today, wearing another of his beautifully tailored suits, this one dark brown with a tie in a matching lighter color.

Nothing like Father, she thought, remembering her father's fondness for comfortable clothes and old cardigans. *But the clothes don't always make the man.*

Henry Ley came to the pulpit to introduce Rev. Golding to the congregation, and barely got the words out before, with visible relief, he took his place in one of the front pews. The minister from North Carolina greeted everyone with a genuine smile and briefly described some of his work in his previous position before starting the service. Bruce Golding had a fine, mellow voice and seemed completely at ease leading the congregation through the familiar passages and responses. He even reminded Louise a little of her father with the friendly way he began his sermon.

"Friends, today I'd like to talk about what God expects of us," Rev. Golding said. He came around the pulpit, carrying his Bible with him, and began walking back and forth as he spoke. "In John 15, Jesus said to his disciples, 'I am the true vine, and my Father is the gardener.'"

"Can't he stay in one spot?" Ethel whispered to Louise.

"It doesn't bother me." Louise thought of Rev. Highland, who had clenched his hands on the sides of the pulpit and leaned over it while he spoke, rapid-fire, like an auctioneer. Now *he* had bothered her.

The visiting minister had barely spoken for five minutes when Louise heard an unhappy whimper a few rows behind her. With a surreptitious glance, she saw that the minister's youngest child was fussing and struggling in her mother's arms. Oddly, Mrs. Golding looked even paler than she had at breakfast.

"As the children of God, we are the branches of that vine," Rev. Golding continued, but he stopped pacing and was obviously watching his wife and baby. "And God wants us to be fruitful and faithful by abiding in Jesus Christ."

She could hear Joyce Golding trying to distract the baby, but the whimpering quickly turned into tears, and the child's cries grew so loud that she nearly drowned out her father's voice.

"Vines produce grapes," the minister said, his face turning red as he made a valiant attempt to speak over his own child's piercing cries. "And so Jesus displays His fruit on His branches, in the way we believe and the lives we live."

Louise, who was particularly sensitive to loud or discordant noises, felt her head begin to pound in time with the baby's wails.

"Why didn't she take them to the nursery?" Ethel murmured to her.

As in most churches, they had a special place set aside for parents with young children, where the kids could make as much noise as they liked. Fred had even set up a speaker so that their parents could listen to the services from there.

Alice overheard her aunt's remark. "I suggested that to her, but she declined," she whispered to Ethel and Louise. "She said she always has the children with her in church back home."

Things only got louder when the other two children decided to chime in and began calling for their father. Although Mrs. Golding tried to calm them, it was only too evident that she was feeling both ill and overwhelmed.

"I'd better go and help her take the children downstairs to the nursery." Alice got up, but Kenneth Thompson stopped her and murmured something. She looked astonished, but nodded hesitantly before slipping out.

As Kenneth also rose and left them to go to the front of the church, Ethel stared. "What does he think he's doing?"

"Looks like he's trying to help," Jane whispered back.

Kenneth spoke in a low voice to Rev. Golding, who gave him a grateful smile before hurrying back to his wife. Kenneth took his position at the pulpit, and regarded the congregation with a serious expression.

"I'm Pastor Kenneth Thompson, visiting from Boston," he introduced himself in a calm, unruffled voice that still carried well over the noise. "As we can see today, sometimes life puts us through trials and tribulations, and they rarely happen at a convenient time."

Louise pressed her fingertips to her throbbing temple. *Tribulations, indeed. That baby's pitch could crack good crystal.*

"But it's in going through these difficulties that we can experience spiritual growth. And if we don't grow, we can't have fruitful lives." There was a particularly sharp cry from the Goldings' baby, and Kenneth nodded toward the child as if in agreement. "We can hear how a little child feels unhappy without her father. It's the same for us. Without the presence of God in our lives, we are just as frightened and lost."

Ethel sat straighter and folded her arms, but like most of the rest of the congregation, she stopped paying attention to the Goldings' children and listened.

"As He said in John 15:5, 'Apart from me you can do nothing,'" Kenneth continued, picking up the theme of his colleague's sermon without a hitch. "We are the branches, but if we separate ourselves from the vine, we bear no fruit."

As soon as their father reached them, the two older children calmed down, and the baby's cries turned to muffled sobs as she buried her little face against her father's jacket. Louise was startled to see Alice with her arm around Mrs. Golding as she led the minister's wife out of the church. Rev. Golding stayed behind with the children, but cast several concerned glances back at where his wife had left with Alice.

"Friends, we don't have to feel alone or unhappy. When we pledge ourselves to be more like Christ, and we allow Him into our hearts, we bloom." Kenneth shared the smiles of the congregation as blessed quiet was restored to the church. "Galatians 5:22–23 tells us, 'The fruit of the Spirit is love, joy, peace, patience, kindness, goodness, faithfulness, gentleness and'—most importantly—'self-control.'"

At that, Rev. Golding chuckled, and so did several other parents present. Louise smiled, until she heard her aunt sniff. Clearly Ethel was not willing to be won over by Rev. Thompson's quick thinking.

"We learn these things from our Father, and from His love for us." Kenneth folded his hands. "Let us pray."

The worshippers bowed their heads.

"Lord, You are the gardener who brings forth all life," he prayed. "We stand before You with open hearts and humbly ask for Your guidance. Hear our prayers, and help us live happy and healthy lives. When we are weak, give us strength and comfort. Teach us the wisdom we need to be better people, and grant us the generosity to help others as they help us. Help us to grow in our faith, and learn to be more like Your Son. Forgive us for our mistakes and failures, and teach us what we need to be Your most fruitful disciples. We praise You through the name of our Lord, Jesus Christ. Amen."

"Amen," the congregation repeated. Many people were watching Kenneth with visible approval now.

The few times it had happened, Louise recalled her father's dealing kindly with crying children during his services. The fact that Kenneth had managed to incorporate the wailing baby as part of his sermon impressed her. As the congregation rose to hear the closing reading, Louise saw that her aunt still radiated disapproval.

"He did very well, don't you think?" she asked in a low voice.

"Oh, he's very smooth, I'll give you that," Ethel said, opening her Bible and holding it so that Louise could read from the page. "A little too smooth for my liking."

One of the ushers came up to speak in a low voice to Rev. Golding, who left at once with the children. The usher then went to the front of the church and whispered something to Kenneth, whose expression went from pleased to serious.

"Friends, I'm going to close the service now and request one more prayer," he said to the congregation. "Rev. Golding's wife Joyce has become very ill, and Alice Howard has taken her to the hospital over in Potterston. Let us pray now for God to watch over her, and to bring her to a swift and full recovery."

After services Louise and Jane drove immediately to the hospital, where they inquired after Mrs. Golding. Hearing that she was stable but had been admitted as an inpatient worried Louise.

"Perhaps I should offer to contact his family back in North Carolina," she said to Jane. She always felt ill at ease near hospitals, and wouldn't have minded going back to the inn. "Her husband will need help with the children if he has returned to Acorn Hill."

"Let's wait until we can talk to Alice—she'll be able to fill us in on Joyce's condition and the family's needs." Jane went to speak to the receptionist.

Alice came down from the wards a few minutes later.

"Everything is fine," she told them. "Mrs. Golding is resting now, and we'll be keeping her overnight for observation."

"Thank the Lord," Jane said. "It's not serious, I hope?"

"She's a little dehydrated and nauseated, but that's to be expected." Her younger sister smiled. "It seems that Joyce is pregnant again, and according to her sonogram, this time she'll be having twins."

"Twins?" The prospect made Louise sit down abruptly. "Good Heavens."

"Believe it or not, she and her husband are thrilled," Alice said. "Rev. Golding told me that they both come from large families, and were hoping the Lord would bless them with the same."

Jane grinned. "He's certainly done that. Speaking of the children, is there someone to take care of the little ones while Joyce is in the hospital?"

"We have them in the pediatric playroom for now, and the nurses and I will look after them. Rev. Golding's parents are on their way and will be here in a few hours to take the children home." Alice checked her watch. "If you don't mind, I'm going to stay until they arrive. The children will be more comfortable with someone they know."

"Call us if you need anything," Jane said.

"I just have to prepare my notes for the church board meeting tomorrow, but that won't take long." Alice gave her a rueful look. "Rev. Golding has decided to stay in North Carolina so his parents can help Joyce when the twins arrive. He's withdrawn his application for the job as head minister for Grace Chapel."

Jane noticed her sister had been more quiet than usual on the way back to the inn from the hospital, and saw her rub her right temple more than once. As they walked up to the porch, she put a hand on her shoulder. "Are you okay, Louise?"

"I just cannot seem to shake this headache." She sighed. "I'll take an aspirin and see if that will help."

They had been so busy with the guests that they had all been working from dawn until dusk without a break, and yet Louise never complained. "Do you want to go lie down for a little while?"

"No, if I take a nap during the day, I will never get to sleep tonight. I'll sit with you in the kitchen for a few minutes, though, if you don't mind."

"Things should be fairly quiet without the children here." Jane went to the front desk. "Let me check the answering machine, and then I'll make us some tea."

When they went into the kitchen a few moments later, Louise noticed the red and white cookbook that Jane had left on the counter. "Is this the cookbook you were telling me about the other day?" She opened the front cover.

"That's it." Jane set the kettle to boil on the stove, then poured a glass of water and retrieved the aspirin bottle she kept in one of the cabinets. "It's something, isn't it?"

"What remarkable names some of these old recipes have." Her sister turned the pages slowly. "I remember a few of them from when I was a child."

"Here." Jane handed her the glass and an aspirin from the bottle. "Guaranteed headache relief, according to the bottle."

"Thank you." Louise took the pill and sipped some of the water. "I did think my head was about to split while we were at church."

"The Goldings' little one certainly has some powerful lungs." Jane studied her sister's face. "That's not the only reason for your headache, though, I think."

"I've never been very comfortable in hospitals," Louise admitted. "Not since Eliot passed away. Maybe it's all the suffering that goes on in them—I don't know how Alice stands it sometimes."

"A lot of good goes on there, too," Jane reminded her.

"That's true. Well, it's not likely that I'll have to go back to one any time soon." She patted the cookbook. "So, what are you planning to do with this?"

"I was thinking of trying out some of the old recipes in it, to give our menu more regional flavor. Look at this." Jane came over and turned to one section in the back. "'The Seven Sweets and Seven Sours.' It seems to be a whole chapter on making homemade pickle relish."

"Back in those days, a housewife had to jar and can everything herself," Louise said. "The 'sweets and sours' are very traditional—the Amish always put out seven of each, especially when they have company."

"What, people counted them?" Jane couldn't help teasing.

"Actually, I believe they did," her older sister said as she turned the page. "It was something of a point of pride. The Amish brought the tradition with them when they emigrated from Germany and Hungary. They made a nice contrast with all the starchy dishes they liked to prepare."

"I think I can skip the sour cherry marmalade," Jane said as she looked over her shoulder, "but those ginger pears sound delicious, and so does that spiced pineapple chutney."

The kettle began to whistle, and Jane went to the stove to prepare the teapot. "It's a shame we can't fit fourteen different relish dishes on the guest tables."

"Two or three would be quite enough, I think." Absorbed by what she was reading, Louise brought the cookbook over to the table, and smiled her thanks for the cup of tea Jane set in front of her. "Oh, look at all the different breads that are here."

"I was also thinking of entering something in the Summer Festival baking contest," Jane said. "Aunt Ethel will be putting in her peach tarts, and I think she needs a little family competition. A regional recipe might get me in good with the judges."

Her sister's mouth curled on one side. "I don't know,

dear, her tarts are almost impossible to beat." She flipped to another section.

Jane leaned over and read some of the recipe headings. "Cherry bread, crusty farm bread, friendship bread." She tapped the page. "Now that sounds interesting."

"It takes ten days to prepare?" Louise rolled her eyes. "Few people are going to feel very friendly toward you if they have to wait that long."

"That allows time for the fruit in the starter to ferment." Jane took the book and studied the recipe. "You know, this just might be a winner. I think I'll try it." On impulse, she reached over and gave her sister a kiss on the cheek.

Louise touched her face, surprised. "What was that for?"

She laughed. "It's just because I love you, silly."

Later that week the board met, and after reading the minutes Alice passed along the news about Rev. Golding's decision to remain in North Carolina.

"I'm sorry to hear that," Lloyd said. "He's a good man, and I enjoyed meeting him."

"That seems like a sensible thing to do," June Carter put in. "It would be very difficult to start in a new ministry and be expecting twins at the same time."

"Which will make, what, seven children?" Florence fanned herself with a folder. "God love the poor woman, I don't know how she'll manage."

Sylvia rolled her eyes. "Imagine just sorting the socks."

"He wouldn't have suited our church anyway." Of all the board members, Ethel appeared the most pleased by Alice's announcement. "The children he has already are too much of a distraction, and you know twins are a full-time job by themselves."

"Seems like we're back to square one again." June looked at Fred. "What's the next step?"

Fred Humbert rubbed his chin. "We still have Pastor Thompson's application to consider. Considering the circumstances, I think he did a fine job of salvaging things at services last Sunday."

"That one? He's nothing like Daniel," Ethel said. "And far too slick, if you ask me. Look at how he tricked that landlord and those tenants."

"Aunt Ethel!" Alice protested. "Pastor Thompson brought those people into the church, and that man to God. He helped them forgive each other."

"That's all well and good, Alice, but he doesn't have any experience working in a smaller, close-knit community like ours," Lloyd said, supporting Ethel's view. "Things are a lot different in Boston than they are here."

"He doesn't have seven children," June said.

"The point is, he's more qualified than any other candidate we've seen." Sylvia sounded rather exasperated. "He gave an excellent interview, and we all saw how well he handled that screaming child at church. He's enthusiastic about living here, and he's a good speaker."

Florence frowned. "What does making a bet with a selfish rich man or talking over a crying baby prove?"

"I think what Sylvia means is that he adapted quickly to an unusual situation." Alice felt very uneasy standing up for the minister, especially as she had liked Rev. Golding more, but she also wanted him to be treated fairly by the board. "It's true that Rev. Thompson hasn't worked in a small town like Acorn Hill, but he wants to. And he did keep services from becoming a disaster."

"He's too standoffish for me." Ethel looked around at the other members of the board, and waved her hand. "Oh, he might be very qualified and know how to give a sermon, but he's nothing compared to Daniel. He's not the man for Grace Chapel."

"No one will ever be like Pastor Howard," Fred said gently. "We can't expect that of anyone, Ethel."

"Of course not." Daniel's sister straightened her shoulders. "Daniel was one in a million."

"We could start over and place a new advertisement in the *Ministry Times*." Sylvia's suggestion made everyone groan. "Well, no one can agree on anyone we've seen so far. What else can we do? We have to find some new candidates."

"We'll just end up arguing over them, too," June predicted in an uncharacteristically gloomy voice.

Everyone looked tired, Alice thought, and she remembered how Louise had warned her that this would happen. She had to do something.

"June is right, finding more candidates won't make a difference." She took a deep breath. "I move that we vote on the remaining candidates under consideration: Rev. Highland, Rev. Winchell and Rev. Thompson."

"S-s-seconded," Henry said, before anyone could object.

Alice gave him a grateful smile.

"Wait a minute, I thought Rev. Winchell didn't want the job," June said.

Sylvia frowned. "Yes, didn't he throw us over for cable TV?"

Lloyd tried to smother a snicker, a bit unsuccessfully. "His wife called a few days ago," the mayor told them. "Seems the good minister's cable show got canceled so that the station could use the time slot for a news talk show. That put her husband back in the running."

"Cyril Overstreet wasn't able to come to the meeting today," Ethel said. "We can't vote without him here."

"According to the church board rules, as long as there are more than two board members present," Fred told her, "we're obligated to vote on a motion."

Ethel glared at Fred as she leaned over and whispered

something in the mayor's ear. Lloyd started to say something, then gave the other board members a sheepish look. Ethel did the same with Florence, who nodded and folded her arms.

Alice cleared her throat. "All in favor of Rev. Highland, please raise your hands."

No one lifted a hand.

Alice hurried on to the next candidate. "All in favor of Rev. Winchell, please raise your hands."

June and Florence voted for the television minister. After a momentary hesitation, so did Lloyd.

Alice saw her aunt give the mayor a tiny nod, and realized what she was doing—she was trying to split up the vote.

"All in favor of Rev. Thompson?" Alice watched as Fred, Henry, and Sylvia raised their hands.

"I'm abstaining and so is Alice, so it's a tie." Ethel looked pleased. "We'll have to make do with what we have."

"No, aunt," Alice said. She thought of her father, and what he would have wanted her to do—the right thing for Grace Chapel. "I will not abstain. I also vote in favor of Rev. Thompson."

"Then it's decided." Fred closed the new candidates file. "We'll offer the position of head minister to Rev. Kenneth Thompson."

Chapter ⛪ Five

"Why on earth would Lloyd vote for Rev. Winchell?" Jane asked that afternoon, as the three sisters sorted and folded the day's wash. "He didn't like him."

"I think Aunt Ethel asked him to, so the vote would deadlock the board." Alice brought over another basket of towels. "She was counting on me not to vote too, I guess."

"At least it is over and done with now." Louise was glad to hear Alice's news about the board's decision to hire Kenneth Thompson. Although she still had her doubts about him, she felt relieved that there would be no more "guest minister" Sundays. She was also impressed that her middle sister had taken her advice and prompted the board into action—she was well aware that forcing people to take action wasn't something that Alice felt comfortable doing.

"With Henry trying to take care of things by himself since Father's been gone, it won't be easy for Kenneth for the first couple of weeks," Jane said. "We should try to help out."

"Rev. Thompson should meet with Henry and the different committees first to discuss the ongoing activities and projects at church." Louise took the basket of bed linens and began matching fitted with folded sheets. "I imagine he will be very busy, no matter what we do."

"I do need to speak to him right away about Vacation Bible School and the Summer Festival," Alice mentioned as she took a towel from her basket and neatly folded it in half, then quarters. "That's only a few weeks from now."

"I know—we could host a reception for him." Jane carried the clean tablecloths over to the linen cupboard and tucked them on a lower shelf. "We could have it right here at the inn, and invite members of the congregation to come and meet the new minister."

"I don't know about that, Jane." Louise neatly stacked the folded bed linens, and then went to place them in an empty basket to carry upstairs. She had to lift out Wendell first, for while they had been talking the tabby had climbed in and settled down for a nap. "He seemed very particular about his schedule. He may want to make his own arrangements."

"I should probably check with the board, too," Alice added as she gave the disgruntled cat a scratch behind the ears. "They may already have something planned." She frowned as she studied the pile she had folded for the kitchen. "I thought we had more hand towels than this."

"I'm sure the board will agree that Grace Chapel Inn is the perfect place to have it." Jane's eyes were shining with pleasure as she expanded on the idea. "I could put something together for this Saturday. Louise, you could provide some musical entertainment—people love to hear you play." She thought for a moment. "Alice, would some of the older kids from your youth group be available to help us with serving?"

"Slow down a minute. We can't have it this Saturday," Alice said as she paired washcloths with their hand towels. "Rev. Thompson will be in Boston for at least another week."

Louise nodded. "He will also have to make arrangements to pack and move his belongings. It might be best to wait until he is settled and learns his way around."

"And maybe it wouldn't." Jane folded her arms and

regarded both of them with obvious disapproval. "You know, I'm beginning to think you two don't like Kenneth."

That surprised Louise. "Don't be ridiculous."

"Of course we like him," Alice added. "He seems like a very nice person."

"Is that right? Then why are you and Louise vetoing every idea I suggest?"

"We simply do not rush headlong into things the way you do, dear," Louise said mildly.

"We're not saying we can't do it, either." Alice consulted the wall calendar. "I suppose we could hold a small reception the weekend after next."

"Is that enough time to make the arrangements and send out proper invitations?" Louise frowned. "That reminds me, Alice, where is the new minister going to be living?"

"Fred has some work to do, clearing out the old rectory, so Kenneth will be staying here at the inn until it's ready," her sister told her. "What kind of reception should we have?"

"I think the question should be, what kind of reception can we afford?" Louise sighed. "This sort of thing can get very costly, and we have to be careful with our budget."

"We could have an afternoon tea," Jane suggested. "It's not as formal or as expensive as a sit-down dinner party. In fact, it would give people more of a chance to talk and mingle."

"That sounds sensible." Louise thought for a moment. "We will need to think about a menu and invitations."

Ethel came through the garden door carrying a round bushel basket of ripe strawberries, dark green zucchini and assorted other vegetables. "I stopped at a farmer's stand and picked up a few things—would you mind making more of your fancy cold vegetable soup, Jane? I'm having Lloyd over to the carriage house for dinner tomorrow night, and it would be perfect with my lemon-herb chicken."

Wendell came over and rubbed his head against the side

of Aunt Ethel's leg as he purred loudly. She was one of his favorite people.

"Yum, can I come over for dinner too?" Jane joked as she admired the vegetables. "Where is this stand? These strawberries are gorgeous, and twice the size of mine."

"I'll take you with me next time. The first cabbages will be out by then." Ethel set the basket on the counter and bent to give Wendell a scratch under the chin, which made the tabby stretch out his neck and close his eyes. "Did I hear you three talking about party invitations? I haven't gone and forgotten someone's birthday, have I?"

Louise noticed Alice's wince, and wondered how much fuss her aunt had been making about the new minister. "We were discussing holding a reception for Kenneth Thompson here at the inn."

Her aunt's smile faded, and she put her purse down on the kitchen table with a slight thump. Sensing trouble, Wendell yawned and wandered out of the kitchen. "Whose idea was this?"

"Mine," Jane said, sounding just as obstinate.

"Really, dear, it's a nice thought, but we hardly know the man."

Louise knew how stubborn her aunt and Jane could be, and decided to step in before they butted heads. "A reception would be a good opportunity for our neighbors to meet the new minister and for us all to get to know him a little better."

"We don't even know if he'll stay at Grace Chapel yet." When Jane glanced over her shoulder, Ethel lifted her chin. "Don't you glower at me like that, Jane Howard. Rev. Thompson is used to living in the city. He may not take to life here in Acorn Hill."

"It would make him feel more comfortable to meet some of the congregation outside of church," Alice suggested. "Didn't the church members hold a reception for Father when he became head pastor?"

Their aunt's forehead wrinkled as she thought for a moment. "No, as I recall, the retiring minister invited Daniel and Madeleine over to his home for dinner." She waved her hand. "You know your father was never one for big parties, anyway."

"We can't afford to throw a big party," Louise said, "but with so many people leaving town on summer vacation, I think we can manage a light buffet and refreshments for twenty or thirty guests."

"You already have enough to do, what with running the inn, and Alice working at the hospital, and Louise giving piano lessons." Ethel shook her head. "It's too much to expect you girls to host something like this."

"If we don't mind, why should anyone else?" Jane said.

The front desk phone rang, and Alice excused herself to answer it.

"Of course, you can do whatever you want." Ethel sounded a little hurt. "Don't mind me."

"We can keep it simple and cozy." Jane came over and put an arm around her aunt's shoulders. "You'll help us, won't you? Everyone knows you make the most delicious peach tarts in the county. Even my best French pastries can't compete with them. We might even have a riot if you don't show up with some."

"I suppose I could make up a few dozen for the guests." She sighed. "All right, Jane, I'll help out—as long as you give me your recipe for that fancy vegetable soup."

Delighted, Jane kissed her cheek. "Deal."

Louise noticed Alice hadn't returned, and went out to the front desk. Her middle sister wasn't on the phone, but the door to their father's study was standing open. She went to the doorway and saw Alice sitting in her father's favorite reading chair, holding a framed picture of Daniel and Madeleine in her hands.

She was lost in thought, and her brown eyes seemed so

sad that Louise almost retreated. But since she had come to live at Grace Chapel Inn with her sisters, she had learned that shared troubles were far easier to manage than troubles endured alone. "Alice?"

Her sister looked up, startled. "Oh, I'm sorry, Louise."

"Are you all right?"

"Yes. I was just thinking about Father and I sort of wandered in here. I do that sometimes." She carefully set the portrait down on the side table next to the chair. "I still miss him."

Louise heard a touch of pain in her younger sister's voice. "That's not all that's bothering you, is it?"

Alice looked down at her hands, and didn't say anything for a few moments. Then she blurted out, "Louise, do you think I did the right thing, casting the deciding vote for Rev. Thompson to be our new minister?"

Naturally she would be worrying about her decision, and all the talk in the kitchen had not helped, Louise realized. She briefly wished Ethel would hurry up and get over her antagonism toward the new minister, for that would go a long way toward eliminating Alice's lingering guilt.

"If you believed that he was the right person for the job, Alice," she told her, "then you did exactly what you should have done."

"I know, it's just that I felt, well, a little disloyal. You know that Aunt Ethel abstained from the voting and expected me to do the same." She twisted her hands together. "Honestly, Louise, I was tempted to."

"But you did what was right instead. C.S. Lewis said, 'Courage is not simply one of the virtues, but the form of every virtue at the testing point.'" Louise walked over and put a hand on her shoulder. "We have all been tested since opening this inn, but it always seems as though you have had more on your shoulders than either Jane or I. I think you have been very brave."

"Not really. I wish Father were here. He always seemed to know exactly the right thing to do." She glanced at her father's image. "What do you think he would have to say about this?"

"Our father would tell you that he's proud of you. I know I am." Louise affectionately smoothed back a short strand of her sister's hair. "You have got a good head on your shoulders, my dear, and a loving heart. No matter what happens, or what anyone else says, never doubt that."

A few days later, Louise had finished preparing the invitations for the reception, and decided to hand deliver a few while she was out doing the weekly shopping. Since the board's decision, word around town was that many people were not happy about the prospect of Kenneth Thompson as the new minister at Grace Chapel.

She was fairly sure her aunt hadn't helped the situation. Far from accepting it, Ethel had done little more than make bleak predictions about the new minister. Because she was Daniel's sister, many people tended to rely on her opinion.

"What if we have this reception and no one shows up? What will the new minister think?" Alice asked after hearing some of the rumors. "I'd go around and see if I could talk some people into attending, but I have my ANGELs meeting tonight, and that gives me so much to prepare."

"Let me go and see what I can do." Louise selected a number of invitations and put them in her purse, then handed the rest to Alice for her to stamp. "I know just where to start, too."

Her sister's mouth curved up. "Viola?"

"Viola."

Louise left the inn early that morning, and walked to the center of town. It was logical to start her campaign to sway popular opinion in favor of the new minister with her friend

Viola Reed. The owner of the Nine Lives Bookstore was, without a doubt, one of the most outspoken, independent people Louise had ever known. There was also no one better, in Louise's opinion, for spreading the word around town that the reception at Grace Chapel Inn was the place to be next weekend.

Now, Louise thought, *how do I convince her to do that?*

The bell above the door jingled as she walked in the shop. Three cats sprawled on Viola's desk lifted their heads to blink sleepily at her before settling back down for another of their endless series of naps.

"I'll be right with you," Viola called out from the back storeroom.

Louise took a moment to admire the latest floor display Viola had arranged. As she did every month, she featured the classic literature she preferred to read, and had arranged a set of Hemingway's complete works along with other books about the Spanish-American War, European travels, and even a slim volume on bullfighting. Viola was determined to present to her customers what she considered "suitable reading," and made no apologies for shelving the current best-sellers off in the corner of the store.

"Hello, Louise." Viola came out of the back carrying two heavy volumes of Milton in one arm and an orange marmalade cat draped over the other. Her bifocals had slipped to the end of her nose, and she was wearing one of her trademark scarves—this one was covered with bright red chili peppers. "Harry got himself stuck in the storeroom again. You'd think after a thousand times he'd learn that he can shut the door, but he can't open it. How are Wendell and your sisters?"

"Jane and Alice are fine, and the cat is just as fat and lazy as ever." Louise smiled; Viola always asked after Daniel's tabby as if he were a person and not a pet. Of course, Viola took care of her own felines better than most people treated their children. "How is business?"

"Don't get me started." Viola put Harry down and took a feather duster from a hook on the wall behind her. "I had a couple of youngsters in here yesterday, wanting comic books." She glowered as she dusted off the two books in her hand. "Bad enough I have to carry best-sellers."

Louise suppressed a smile. "Did you call the police?"

"I was tempted, Louise. I was tempted." Viola flicked the duster over her desk, and one of the cats reached out and batted it with a lazy paw. "I told them they were too old to be looking at picture books and let them borrow one of my Narnia novels." The bookshop owner kept a box of "lender" copies of classic literature specifically for the children in town, as few had enough pocket money to buy the books. She saw it as an investment in the future.

"An excellent choice. That cookbook that you gave to Jane has her in raptures, by the way. She's already started experimenting on some sort of bread that takes ten days to make." Louise rolled her eyes. "She's determined to give Aunt Ethel some competition in this year's baking contest."

Viola shook her head. "I've had some of Ethel's peach tarts. She hasn't a snowball's chance in Hades against them."

"Don't tell her that." Since her friend seemed to be in a fairly good mood, Louise took out the envelope addressed to Viola and handed it to her. "I stopped in to deliver an invitation to our reception for Rev. Thompson next weekend."

"I heard about him from your aunt." The faint emphasis she placed on *him* made it obvious she hadn't heard anything good. "I don't think I can make it." Viola set the envelope on her desk.

"Are you busy?" Louise raised her eyebrows. "Do you have a prior engagement?"

"Only with my hair dryer." Her bifocals glinted as she shook her head. "I'm sorry, Louise. It's just, I don't think much of this new minister."

"Indeed!" Louise folded her hands together. "And on

what have you based that opinion? Other than my aunt's opinion, I mean—have you even met the man yet?"

"He came in here while he was staying in town." Viola gestured toward the best-seller rack. "I made my usual recommendations, but all he bought was a historical mystery novel and a nonfiction travel guide."

Louise reined in her temper, which under the circumstances required near-heroic strength. "Viola, you cannot judge a man for buying two books that you didn't like."

"I've always maintained that you can tell a great deal about a person by what he reads." The bookstore owner flicked the duster over a nearby shelf. "A minister with a good education would appreciate the classics more."

"Rev. Thompson was just visiting when he was here last. He probably has a whole library of classics at home," Louise protested. "Viola, please. You really should give the man a fair chance."

"*Hmmm.*" She dusted off another row of books. "You've always been insightful about people, Louise. What do you think of him?"

"I don't know Rev. Thompson very well, but I saw at services how he handles difficult situations, and he's obviously very intelligent and articulate," she said, realizing just then how little she really did know about the new minister. "I would like to get to know him better before I form an opinion."

Viola chuckled with appreciation. "Meaning so should I."

"If the shoe fits."

"The shoe doesn't bother me as much as some other things." She straightened the spine of one book and faced out another. "Sylvia said the suits he wears are hand-tailored, you know. That sounds pretty high maintenance to me."

"Or he's the kind of man who buys a few good suits instead of a lot of cheap ones." Louise picked up a first edition of *The Old Man and the Sea* that had a rather unattractive dust jacket. "You wouldn't judge this book by its cover art."

"True." The bookshop owner considered that for a few moments, then finally nodded. "All right, I'll come to your reception." She looked over her bifocals at Louise. "I'm not promising anything, you understand—and I'm not *joining* anything."

Louise thanked her friend and left the bookstore to cross Hill Street and walk over to Acorn Avenue, to drop off an invitation at Sylvia's Buttons. The dressmaker was busy with a rush order to alter an exquisite satin and lace wedding dress, but she was happy to be invited and promised to be there.

"I know just the outfit I want to wear, I was altering the sleeves on it only last week," Sylvia talked around the pins in her mouth as she tacked a ruffle onto the sweeping hem of the voluminous gown. She glanced around the crowded confines of her little shop. "If I can find it again."

From there Louise headed to the Coffee Shop, where she intended to rest her feet and speak with Hope Collins and June Carter. She felt sure June would attend, but it was Hope she needed to sway. Hope was almost as adept as Viola at spreading information around Acorn Hill.

Unfortunately, June was visiting relatives in Potterston for the day, and Ethel had been to the Coffee Shop ahead of Louise. Hope seemed even more reluctant to commit herself than Viola had been.

"I can't speak for June, but I'm not sure I can make it, Louise," Hope said, avoiding her gaze as she filled Louise's water glass and handed her a menu. "The weekends are my only days off, and I have a lot to do around the house."

"You don't have to stay long," Louise suggested as she studied the list of sandwiches. "If you can stop in for a few minutes to say hello to Rev. Thompson, that will be fine."

"I've already met him." Hope glanced at the counter to check on her other customers, and then slid into the booth, across the table from Louise. "He came in here a couple of times while he was in town."

She put down the menu. "Then you won't mind helping us welcome him as our new minister."

"The thing is . . . I'm just not too sure about him. You don't think he's a little slick, like your aunt says?" Hope asked.

Louise tried not to grit her teeth as she smiled. *Aunt Ethel, you and I are going to have to have a little talk.* "Goodness, no. He's simply very decisive and self-confident. I think those are important assets, especially for a minister. He will be providing the spiritual guidance for our church members, and he cannot do that if he's the shy and retiring type."

"I suppose that's true." Hope seemed to waver. "If he was only a little more like Pastor Howard, but he's so different. So . . . standoffish." She glanced at the counter, then added in a slightly indignant whisper, "He doesn't even *like* blackberry pie!"

Louise thought of how her father had walked into town on a regular basis to have a slice of his favorite treat. "Well, Hope, I'm not very fond of blackberry pie myself. Does that mean I should move back to Philadelphia?"

The waitress's response was immediate. "Land sakes no. You grew up here in Acorn Hill."

A light went off inside Louise's head. *Of course, that is the key.* "But you didn't," she gently reminded the waitress. "Hope, you know how it feels to move to a new place where you don't know everyone. Imagine how hard it would be if everyone was actively avoiding you. Do you still remember the first month you spent here in Acorn Hill?"

"It *was* hard, the first couple of weeks," Hope admitted in a low voice. "I never thought of it like that."

"It's easier to make friends when someone is willing to meet you halfway."

She looked down at the invitation, and her expression softened. "Rev. Thompson does seem to like apple pie. Maybe I could bring one for him, as a welcoming gift?"

"I think that would be a lovely thing to do," she said gently. "Thank you, Hope."

Louise had a light brunch at the Coffee Shop before finishing her rounds. Some others she spoke to also showed a reluctance to attend, but by applying the same logic as she had with Hope and Viola, she managed to talk them around.

Her last stop was at Acorn Hill Antiques, but before she crossed the street she waited for a blue sedan to pass. The car looked slightly familiar, but passed too quickly for her to make out who was driving it.

Inside the antique shop, she found Joseph Holzmann unpacking his latest shipment.

"Good afternoon, Louise," he greeted her. He was a short, thin man who wore a neat beard and old-fashioned, gold-rimmed glasses. "What can I do for you?"

"I've come to invite you and your wife to our reception for the new minister at Grace Chapel." She took a moment to admire the beautiful Meissen clock he had carefully extracted from a well-padded box. The old porcelain timepiece was adorned with cherubs and flowers fashioned and hand painted in the ornate Baroque style. "Oh, Joseph, that's lovely."

"Some of the flowers were chipped and had to be professionally restored." He turned it over to reveal a marking of crossed swords under the glaze. "The customer will be very pleased—the artisan did a fine job."

Rachel Holzmann came out of the back office carrying something wrapped in terry cloth that had a distinctive red and black striping. "Joseph, I've found the fair market value in the appraiser's catalog, but I'd like to call Mr. Alcott—" she halted when she saw the two of them. "Why, hello, Louise." She put down what she was carrying on one of the tables. "We haven't seen you for some time."

Louise explained the reason for her visit, and the couple gladly accepted the invitation.

"Is there anything we can bring?" Joseph asked.

"Not that I can think of, Joseph."

"Dear, remember that we must get everything cataloged today." Rachel gave her husband a direct look as she took Louise's arm and guided her toward the front of the shop. "We're in such a rush—we're going to Europe for the summer, and there are a thousand things to do before we leave."

As she headed back toward the inn, Louise felt slightly uneasy. Rachel Holzmann had given her such an odd look when she had first seen her standing there, and then had almost rushed her out of the shop. It was almost as if Joseph's wife didn't feel comfortable having her there.

There was also something else nagging at the back of her mind—a feeling that something else was not quite right. But what could it be?

Chapter ✤ Six

Alice arranged her work schedule to keep time available for her weekly ANGELs meeting at church. The ANGELs were a group of girls whose ages ranged from eleven to fourteen; they were the focal point of Alice's work in youth ministry.

Using the Assembly Room at church gave the group plenty of workspace for their studies and for the different projects the group planned. Since one of the topics to be discussed at the meeting was the Summer Festival, Alice had invited some older children from the church's youth group to join them. After leading prayer and a short Bible study session, Alice distributed copies of the summer meeting schedule and the tentative schedule for Fourth of July weekend.

"We need to decide tonight what we're going to do for the Summer Festival," she reminded the children. "Mayor Tynan wants to finish the schedule this week."

The whole town participated in the annual Acorn Hill Summer Festival, held over the Independence Day holiday, and the ANGELs were particularly eager to take part.

"A field day would be fun," one of the girls suggested. "We could have sack races and water balloon tosses."

"But we're already doing a sports day the week before, during Vacation Bible School," another protested.

"We could have a carnival," Sissy Matthews, Louise's prized piano student, suggested. "We could make up the games and sell tickets like we did last summer. We raised almost two hundred dollars for our outreach mission."

"I want to do something different this year." Charles Matthews, always at odds with his older sister, glared in her direction. That he was present only because his ANGEL sister was acting as his baby-sitter for the evening in no way fazed the ten-year-old.

Several of the older kids from the youth group chimed in to agree with Charles.

"Perhaps I could suggest some ideas?" a familiar voice asked.

Startled, Alice looked up to see the new minister standing in the doorway. "Pastor Thompson! I didn't know you were back in town."

"I just arrived today. I saw the lights on in the church as I drove by. I hope I'm not interrupting." He looked at the group with interest.

"No, of course not." She put down her notebook and rose to her feet. "Children, this is Pastor Kenneth Thompson, our new head pastor." She went around the room, introducing each child by name.

Kenneth smiled. "I'm very pleased to meet you."

As the kids chorused a hello, he came in and gestured toward an empty chair at Alice's right. "Would you mind if I sit in on the rest of your meeting?"

"Not at all." She pulled out the chair. "We were just discussing how we'd like to participate in the annual Summer Festival." She handed him a copy of the tentative program. "There are already a lot of events scheduled."

"*Hmm*, there are." He studied the list. "Have you thought about putting on an evening program at church?" he asked Alice.

"A musical program, like we do at Christmas time?" one of the girls asked.

"Music is always good entertainment," Kenneth said, "but I was thinking more along the lines of a drama. Has your group ever put on a play?"

"I think some of the children have been in plays at school, and we've done skits for Vacation Bible School." Alice thought for a moment. "But I don't think we've put on a formal play at church since I was a girl."

"That must have been a long time ago," Bobby Dawson, one of the boys from the youth group, said.

Alice laughed. "A *very* long time ago."

"What kind of play could we do?" Sissy Matthews asked.

Kenneth promptly turned the question around. "There are many great stories in the Bible. Which ones are your favorites?"

Although he was obviously not as comfortable with the children as her father had been, Alice was pleased to see that he listened to the different suggestions made by the youngsters. He also didn't try to talk down to them, something she had almost expected him to do.

"There should be a theme that relates to this time of year," Kenneth prompted. "What do you all like to do during the summer?"

"Play baseball!" several of the boys said together.

"We have lots of picnics and cookouts," a girl added.

"I go fishing at the creek with my dad every weekend," Charles Matthews said. "Mom always cooks what we catch for dinner."

"*Yuck!*" His sister wrinkled her nose. "And Dad makes him clean them."

All of the ANGELs groaned, while the boys eyed Charles with admiration.

"I think you've got something there, Charles," the minister said. "In Chapter Four of the Book of Matthew, Jesus called the first of His disciples, and they were fishermen. Does anyone know those verses?"

One of the older girls raised her hand, and when Kenneth nodded to her, flipped through the pages of her Bible and then read: "As Jesus was walking beside the Sea of Galilee, he saw two brothers, Simon called Peter and his brother Andrew. They were casting a net into the lake, for they were fishermen. 'Come, follow me,' Jesus said, 'and I will make you fishers of men.' At once they left their nets and followed him."

"There are a lot of other good stories about fish and fishermen in the Bible, too," Alice put in. "I think that would make a wonderful theme for a play."

"Would you help us write it, Pastor?" Bobby asked.

Alice felt a little embarrassed. "I think Pastor Thompson will be too busy for that, Bobby."

"I'm never that busy," Kenneth assured the boy, then looked at Alice. "I'd be happy to come and work with the children during your next meeting, if that's all right."

Alice nodded, but she felt a small amount of dismay. Since her father's death, Henry Ley had offered to help with her youth ministry, but aside from his asking parents for donations for their various projects, she had done almost everything with the youngsters by herself—particularly any projects involving the ANGELs, as they were her special concern. Before that, the Summer Festival had always been a project that Alice had worked on with her father.

"We'd be grateful for your assistance, Pastor," she said at last. "That wraps up the meeting for tonight, kids. Pastor, would you lead us in closing prayer?"

Alice had walked to the church for the meeting, but after the last child had been picked up and she had locked the church doors, she found Kenneth waiting outside for her and accepted his offer of a lift.

"How long have you been working with youngsters?" he asked as he drove the short distance from the church to the inn.

"Quite some time now. I founded the ANGELs in the distant past . . . about the same time the wheel was invented."

He chuckled in response. "I enjoyed joining in with your discussion—they're a very bright group. I haven't had much opportunity to work with children."

"My father always said that the trick to working with kids is to encourage, not discourage." As Kenneth parked in the drive, she hesitantly added, "If you're not comfortable with working with the youth, Pastor . . ." she wasn't sure quite how to put it. "What I mean is, please don't feel obligated to get involved. I know you have a great deal more to do."

"Actually, Miss Howard, I'm looking forward to it." He walked around and opened the door for her.

Alice thanked him for the lift as they strolled inside. As he went upstairs to his room, she went to the kitchen, where she found Jane taking a large pan of odd-looking muffins from the oven.

The tantalizing aroma of warm strawberries made her sniff the air with appreciation. "Are those for the guests or for us? Please say us."

"These are an experiment. I made some oatmeal raisin bars earlier, if you're hungry." Jane nodded toward the golden brown squares she'd stacked on a plate on the counter.

Alice studied the pan. "You're experimenting on our guests?"

"Well, you and Louise don't volunteer to be my guinea pigs." Jane gave her a teasing wink. "These are strawberry popovers. I'm going to drizzle them with a new yogurt sauce I found in a magazine. If it works, we'll have them at the reception."

"Oh, Father would have loved these. I remember how Mother used to make popovers for him." Alice made a rueful face. "I tried her recipe once, but mine didn't pop. They turned out more like chewy, golden hockey pucks." She picked up one of the oatmeal raisin bars and bit into it with delight. She didn't notice the odd look her younger sister gave her as she snitched a second bar from the plate. "If they don't work out, these are good, too."

⚬⚬

After Alice left the kitchen, Jane put her experimental popovers on a cooling rack and went out into the garden. She had to get out of the kitchen for a few minutes; she had been in there for so long it felt like the walls were closing in on her. And after all her fiddling with the old popover recipe, the heat of the oven had made her a bit lightheaded.

Oh, Father would have loved these.

During the renovation of the old house, Fred Humbert had done considerable work in the garden, including the installation of photo-sensitive lights along the garden paths, so that any guests who wanted to stroll outside after dark would be able to find their way around. One of the lights partially lit some bold pink clematis that she was trying to train to one of the three white wood trellises curving over the garden path.

I remember how Mother used to make popovers for him.

Daniel had never seen the trellises; they had also been a new addition, like the garden path lights. He would never see what Jane had done with the flower beds and the rows of vegetables on the other side of the yard. He would never taste one of her strawberry popovers, or any of the dishes that she had made for hundreds of strangers who came to eat at the restaurant where she had worked. Whenever she had come home on one of her rare visits, Daniel had always insisted on doing the cooking.

"You're on vacation," he would say. "A chef on vacation is not allowed *near* a stove."

It wasn't as if her sisters had pampered their father with exotic dishes, either. *I tried her recipe once, but mine didn't pop. They turned out more like chewy, golden hockey pucks.*

Alice had joked about the quality of her own cooking, but at least she had been here for their father. At least she had tried.

Some stray dandelions had sprouted up in the bed, and Jane knelt down to tug them out. Then she saw the patch of chickweed creeping out from under the clematis, and went after that. She was so intent on her weeding that she didn't hear the footsteps behind her.

"Good evening, Jane."

She looked up to see Kenneth Thompson standing beside her. "Hello, Pastor. Did you need something?"

"I thought I'd come out for some fresh air." He looked around. "I didn't have a chance to see the garden properly the last time I was here. It's lovely."

"You can see it better during the daylight." She looked down at her hands, which were trembling slightly, then stood up. "We have a little table set up for guests, if you'd like to have your breakfast out here tomorrow."

"I think I'd enjoy that." He looked down at the mound of weeds she had pulled from the bed. "Do you often work out here at night?"

Jane glanced quickly at him. She was inclined toward anger, but his expression showed only polite interest. Her ex-husband would have jumped at the chance to ridicule her for losing her temper, of course.

Not every man is like Justin, she reminded herself. *He's only trying to be nice.*

"No, generally I wait until after breakfast." She brushed bits of soil and leaves from her trousers. "I guess I spent too much time closed up in the kitchen today. I felt like I was getting a case of cabin fever."

"Would you mind sitting with me for a moment?" He nodded toward one of the conversation benches lining the path. "I'd appreciate your company."

She usually enjoyed sitting and chatting with someone,

but tonight she only wanted to be alone. Good manners forced her to reply, "Of course I don't mind."

After they sat down, he told her about the plans he and Alice had made with the ANGELs and the youth group for the Summer Festival. Jane tried to be attentive, but she found it hard to concentrate on what he was saying. She kept smelling the faint odor of strawberries from the kitchen, and seeing her father's kind face.

Did you hate me for staying away, Father? She couldn't bear it if he had.

Kenneth interrupted her reflections when he asked her something, and she missed the entire question. "I'm sorry," she said. "My mind was wandering."

"I asked if you had a garden plan, or if you followed the original schematic for planting."

"I tried to restore the garden to what it was, but I also added a few things here and there." She looked at a night-blooming jasmine bush nearby. "I don't think my father would recognize it now." *Would he have approved?* She would never know.

"He would value the work you've put into transforming it," Kenneth said, as if reading her mind.

"It's really too little, too late." She twisted the copper bracelet she wore.

"Why do you feel that way?"

Putting it into words was difficult for her, but she suspected she would feel better if she got them out. "Now that Father's gone, it doesn't matter what I do. I should have come home more often and spent time with him, but I was always so busy with my husband and my career. I visited him only rarely over the years. Now I have no husband, no career, and my father will never see anything I do."

He was silent for a minute and then said, "I do know how you feel." He removed his wallet from his jacket, and took a small photo of a smiling young woman from it. "This is my wife, Catherine. She died quite suddenly ten years ago, from a heart condition."

Jane took the photo and studied it. "She was a beautiful woman."

"She was, as well as the gentlest person I've ever known." He looked out at the garden. "I still think about all the things we could have done, if we had had more time together."

"You must have loved her very much." Jane looked at the picture and felt terribly guilty for reminding him of his own bereavement. Carefully she handed it back to him. "I'm so sorry for your loss."

"Thank you. When I met Catherine, we were both in college. Unlike me, she was deeply involved in charity work. She was the one who showed me how a life of service was truly a worthwhile calling." He tucked the photo away and replaced his wallet. "She taught me to live what I believe."

Jane recalled words from years before. "My father said a life without true purpose was a waste of God's valuable time and material. Maybe I could have done more with mine, if I'd come back home a long time ago."

"Did your father ever ask you to move back to Acorn Hill?"

"No, not once. He knew how much I wanted to travel and see some of the world. He never asked me for anything." She shrugged. "It wasn't as if he was stuck here all alone, either. He had Alice living here with him, and Louise visited a few times a year." She swallowed hard. "I think he was happy."

"But you're not."

"No," she admitted. "Alice said things—nothing unkind—but what she said reminded me of all the things I could have done for my father. Things that I'll never be able to do now. I could have been a better daughter to him, Kenneth. I could have tried harder."

"If only we could change the past, but . . ." He turned to her, his expression grave. "Jane, your father wouldn't want you to feel guilty about this."

"I know, but he was a minister." She looked up toward heaven, and wondered if her father was watching her have this little selfish tantrum. "He forgave everyone, no matter what they did."

"A father's love is like God's love. It's not conditional." He took her hand in his. "Yes, he was a minister, but he was your father first."

She grimaced. "And I'm the classic prodigal daughter."

"Did you cut off all contact with him while you were away?" he asked.

"No, we wrote letters to each other and talked on the phone quite often between my visits." She smiled, remembering some of the conversations she had had with Daniel in the past. "Father always seemed interested in hearing about the places I went, and my work, and the people I met. He said he got a vicarious thrill from hearing about my adventures."

"And do you believe that he resented your leaving home?"

"No. He never even hinted about anything like that." She shook her head. "Still, I could have tried to be more like Louise and Alice. It would have made him happier in his last years."

"I didn't know your father, but from what I've heard about him, he was not a selfish man. He would not have wanted his children to live identical lives or stay here to please him." Kenneth smiled. "He would have wanted you to be the individuals that you are."

She ducked her head. "When I came home for his funeral, I found a bundle of letters in his desk. Do you know, he saved every single letter I'd ever written to him?"

"It sounds to me as if he loved you very much."

She nodded quickly, still not meeting his gaze. "I've never doubted that he did."

"More than anything, I believe parents want their children to live up to their full potential, even if that potential means having to let them go out into the world and find their place in it." His gentle voice made her look up at him. "I think your father understood this because it's also what God expects of us. By His grace, He gave us eternal encouragement and hope, so that we can be strong and courageous in our words and our deeds—whether we stay at home or we travel to the ends of the earth."

Thinking about it from that perspective made Jane feel a sense of relief. "Thank you, Pastor."

"You're welcome." Kenneth rose and glanced at the kitchen. "Now, can I convince the chef of Grace Chapel Inn to let me try whatever smells so wonderful in the kitchen?"

"I think that can be arranged," Jane said as she got up and walked back with him to the kitchen. "How do you feel about being a guinea pig?"

Louise had just gone to bed the night before when she heard voices coming from the garden, and looked out to see Jane and Kenneth Thompson sitting on one of the garden benches. She didn't want to listen in on their conversation, but it was clear from Jane's expression that she was upset about something. She intended to ask her youngest sister about it over breakfast the next morning, but Alice brought the matter up first.

"What were you and Pastor Thompson talking about for so long in the garden last night, Jane?" Alice poured a cup of tea for her sister, who had just finished reading her section of the newspaper. "You were out there for almost an hour."

"We just discussed a few things." Jane set the paper aside

and looked at both of her sisters. "Did Father ever say anything to either of you about wanting me to come back home?"

Louise was surprised. "Well he missed you, of course, but no, he never said anything like that."

"He was so proud of everything you did," Alice added. "He kept all your letters, and a scrapbook with all the pictures and postcards you sent."

Jane frowned. "I found the letters when I was looking through his desk for some insurance papers, but I never saw any scrapbook."

"That can't be—it was in the same drawer, right under the letters. I'll go and get it." Alice rose and left the kitchen.

Louise was also puzzled. "I don't recall seeing a scrapbook in the desk, and I went through all of Father's papers just a few weeks ago."

Jane glanced at her wrist. "You know, this is strange. Last week I couldn't find my watch. I usually leave it on the counter when I go out to the garden, but I thought I'd taken it off and left it somewhere else. Then it turned up one morning, right next to the coffee maker. And you know, I'm almost positive I didn't see it there the night before, and I wiped down all the counters myself right after dinner."

Louise thought of her Bible, and wondered if she could have picked up her sister's watch and moved it. "I don't remember seeing it there either, Jane," she said.

Alice returned with a large scrapbook in her hands. "I found it. It was on the shelf next to Father's chair." She seemed troubled by that.

"Did you put it there, Alice?" Jane asked.

"No, I left everything in his desk the way it was." Alice placed the scrapbook on the table. "Louise, you said you didn't see this, and neither did Jane. That means someone has been in Father's desk."

"Okay, now I know something funny is going on," Jane

said. "Have either of you noticed anything else missing around here in the last couple of weeks?"

"I misplaced my Bible, but I found it a few days later on the piano in the parlor," Louise said. The only problem was, she did not remembering taking it into the parlor at all.

"There are some kitchen towels missing from the wash," Alice mentioned. "And I did notice that someone moved two of the hospitality dishes from the reception desk to the study."

"It's probably one of the guests," Jane said.

"But why would one of the guests go through the desk, and why move this?" Alice placed her hand on the cover of the scrapbook. "What would they be looking for?"

Louise disliked the idea of suspecting their guests almost as much as thinking it was her own fault that things were being shuffled around and misplaced. "We have been very trusting about the people who stay with us. Perhaps we better keep a closer eye on things for the time being."

"Good idea." Jane began paging through the scrapbook. "Look at this, Father really did save all this stuff." She sounded pleased.

"Of course he did. He loved to show it to people, too." Alice sat down beside her younger sister, and turned the pages to the middle of the book. "See this?" She carefully unfolded a newspaper clipping. "This is an article about the restaurant where you worked. Fred brought the paper back for Father after he and Vera went to California on vacation."

"I remember this one." Jane made a face. "Justin and I had a huge argument over it. He felt the critic was being too nice about my seafood dishes. Of course, the same critic wrote up his chicken à la king and said he'd tasted better chicken in a fast food restaurant."

Louise exchanged a glance with Alice. Jane rarely referred to her ex-husband, but when she did, her words usually revealed a touch of dejection. "Perhaps Justin was a little jealous."

"Oh, Justin was *unquestionably* jealous—that's one of the reasons we got divorced, I'm sad to say. He always felt he had to compete with me to see who was the better chef. Then when the better chef turned out to be me, he couldn't stand it." Jane closed the scrapbook. "May I keep this up in my room for a few days? I'd like to look through it when I have more time."

"Certainly. Perhaps you'd better keep it there until we discover why things keep getting moved around." As she heard one of the guests coming downstairs, Louise finished her tea. "I better go out to the dining room."

Chapter ⛪ Seven

The day of the reception arrived, and the final preparations kept all three of the Howard sisters busy from the moment they awoke. Louise had decided on what music she wanted to play and sat down to practice that morning. Meanwhile, Jane remained stationed in the kitchen, watching over the final batches of baking while making up the fancy fruit and vegetable platters for the buffet. Alice divided her time three ways: at the front desk, in the dining room and in the parlor, which required considerable effort to set up for the reception.

Alice didn't realize she was humming along to the lovely music coming from the piano until Trent Alcott commented on it as he came down for breakfast.

"Isn't it a bit early for a concert?" the estate buyer asked.

"We're having a reception for our new minister this afternoon, and my sister is providing the music," Alice explained as she filled his cup. She looked at the empty chair beside him. "Should I take a tray up for Mrs. Alcott?"

"No, Mother will be down later."

"I hope she's feeling well?"

"Mother is under the weather quite a lot these days, and sometimes you might find that she gets a bit . . . confused."

He eyed the teapot she set on the table, which had delicate pale green flowers detailed against a creamy peach-pink background, and matched the sugar and creamer on his table. "You know, I have a client who collects Wedgwood wildflower pieces exclusively. He would probably pay at least three hundred dollars for just this teapot."

Alice had gotten used to the estate buyer's interest in buying things around the inn. "That's something to consider, Mr. Alcott, but then how would I pour your tea?"

He gave her a shrewd look. "You could buy a lot of teapots with three hundred dollars, Ms. Howard. Ones you could afford to replace if anything ever happened to them."

That reminded Alice of the cameo vase she had broken. "Thank you for the offer, but we're very fond of the ones we already have." She took his order, and then went to the kitchen. "Jane, Mr. Alcott only wants a poached egg and toast this morning. His mother isn't feeling well and will be down a little later."

"No problem." Jane looked up from the omelet she was filling with diced ham and vegetables. "Would you get two more plates down from the cabinet for me, Alice?"

Alice took down the plates and set them within easy reach on the counter, then began slicing grapefruit. "He also wants to buy our Wedgwood teapot."

"Mr. Alcott wants to buy everything we own." Jane flipped one half of the omelet over onto itself. "Just last week he offered me seven hundred and fifty dollars for that set of silver hospitality dishes we have out in the parlor. You know, those little dishes we keep candy in?"

"I didn't know they were worth so much."

Jane shrugged. "Why people would pay that kind of money for some old used dishes is beyond me. Should we stick little Not For Sale signs on everything?"

"No, but I can't blame Mr. Alcott. Buying antiques is his job, and we do have some lovely old things." Alice gnawed at her bottom lip. "Jane, do you think it would cost a lot of money to replace that vase that I broke?"

Jane stared at her as if startled, then blinked. "What vase are you talking about?"

"You remember, the green cameo vase. The one from the matching set that Father gave to Mother for their anniversary." She added grapefruit to the plates, then held one out as Jane expertly removed the omelet from the pan. "I still feel terrible about that."

"I don't know how much it would cost, but I think you'd have a very hard time even finding a replacement," Jane said. "That vase was over sixty years old."

"You're right. I don't have time to look, either." Alice sighed, then brightened. "I know—what if I showed the other one to Mr. Alcott? He's an expert on antiques. Maybe he could tell me where I could find a match." She looked around. "Only I haven't seen the other one. Do you know where it is?"

"One of us might have stored it away someplace safe during the renovations, but I think we should look for it another time." Jane went to the refrigerator to take out a block of cheese. "Today we've got to concentrate on the reception."

"Right." The bell at the front desk rang. "That will be Fred with the extra tables for the parlor. I'll be back in just a minute."

"Don't rush," her sister told her. "I can take Mr. Alcott's order out to him."

Once Louise felt satisfied with her musical arrangement, she went to work on arranging the floral centerpieces for the tables. She had always enjoyed working with flowers, and although the results were perhaps not quite as professional as a florist's would have been, using flowers from their own garden added a satisfying touch of color to the room. As she worked, Alice and Fred set up three sturdy folding tables, which Louise draped with lace-edged white linen cloths.

"These look very nice," Alice said as she arranged the last of the centerpieces beside the buffet trays. "I might steal one for the front desk after the reception."

"If you do, let me know so I don't think one of the guests has taken it somewhere," Louise joked.

"That reminds me." She told her older sister about her idea to replace the green cameo vase and then asked, "Have you seen the other vase around here anywhere?"

"Why no, I don't believe I have." Louise inspected the tables with a critical eye, and then straightened the edge of one cloth. "I think it is a lovely idea, and I agree Mr. Alcott could be quite helpful, but you will have to find the matching vase first."

Alice glanced at the mantel. "No time . . . to hunt for it . . . today . . ." She frowned. The old brass-faced clock that had always occupied the center of the mantel above the fireplace was gone. "Louise, did you take the old mantel clock out of here?"

"No, I did not." After looking around, Louise spotted the mantelpiece clock in one of the curio cabinets. "There it is."

Alice went over with her to the cabinet. The figurines that usually occupied the center shelf had been carefully moved aside and arranged around the old clock.

"What on earth is it doing in here?" She opened the door to take the clock out and returned it to its proper place. "We have always kept the clock on the mantel."

Louise felt terrible. If she was having a problem with her memory, obviously it was time to tell her sisters about it. "Alice, I think this could be my fault."

"You moved it there?"

"I might have." She sat down on the piano bench. She could not keep this to herself, not after seeing the clock. "I have been getting very absentminded lately. I keep forgetting where I put my things. Just last week I misplaced the Bible

Eliot gave to me when we were married. I thought I had it in my room, but it was gone, and then I found it on the piano a few days later. I do not remember leaving it there."

Alice looked astonished. "That doesn't sound like you at all. You've always been very careful with your things, even when we were girls. Remember how you used to keep count of your socks, and arrange them in your drawer by size and color?"

"We're not girls any longer." Louise gripped the edge of the seat. "Oh, Alice, I was afraid I would start doing this when I got older." She gave her a miserable look. "What if there is something wrong with me?"

"I think you're mistaken. Father was never absent-minded, and neither is Aunt Ethel. I also think Jane and I would have noticed before this," Alice assured her. "If it's anyone, it's me—after all, we have to set the clocks ahead five minutes just to get me out of here on time. Or it could be Jane. You know how she gets when she's busy in the kitchen—all she thinks about is what's cooking."

"Just the same, maybe I should make an appointment and have some tests done." Louise glanced at the piano. Over her lifetime she had learned so many lovely pieces of music by heart. Would she lose them now? And what about Eliot? All she had left of him were her memories of their happy years together. "I'll call the doctor's office on Monday."

Ethel and Lloyd Tynan were the first to arrive for the reception. Their aunt wore a very feminine white eyelet dress with blue ribbon bows on the sleeves, and matched Lloyd, who was wearing one of his white suits and a blue bow tie. After taking two containers with her famous peach tarts in to Jane, she volunteered to man the front desk.

"I'll look after the phone while you and Alice change for the party," she told Louise. "Is Rev. Thompson here yet?"

Louise checked the time. "No, but we expect him very shortly."

Ethel sniffed. "I certainly hope he's not late for his own reception."

Louise stopped in the kitchen, but Jane had already dressed for the reception, protecting her vivid flowery dress with a large apron. She was setting out Ethel's tarts onto a large oval platter and keeping a close eye on her strawberry popovers, the last batch of which were still in the oven.

"They're best served warm, so I left them to the last minute," she told her, shooing her out through the door. "Go on, get dressed. I've got everything here under control."

Up in her room, Louise tried to forget about the troubling incident with the clock and selected one of her classic summer crepe dresses in a flattering shade of powder blue. She added a single short strand of pearls and matching earrings, and inspected herself in the mirror.

The pleasure she took in dressing up faded as she studied her silvery hair and the fine network of lines around her eyes. She had never thought of herself as an old woman, but perhaps it was time to face the fact that she was.

"Classics never become dated," Eliot had always said. "You always dress as you play, my dear, always with the lightest touch of elegance and style."

Someone knocked at her bedroom door, and in the reflection she saw Alice peek in. "Are you almost ready?"

"Almost." She beckoned to her. "Come in for a minute."

"I love that color on you." Alice rarely wore dresses herself, but for the occasion had put on a chestnut-colored linen skirt and a crisply tailored ivory blouse. "How do I look?"

Louise eyed her. "Very pretty, but that blouse needs a necklace." She went to her jewelry box and took out a double strand of tiger-eye beads. The golden-brown shimmer of the stones complemented Alice's skirt, eyes and hair. "Here, this will go perfectly."

Alice put it on and checked her reflection. "Oh, it does, thank you." She met Louise's gaze in the mirror. "You're not nervous, are you?"

"No."

"Then why the sad look?"

"I was just thinking about Eliot." She forced a smile. "We should go downstairs before the guests start arriving."

Louise was pleased to see Kenneth Thompson arrive, and she accepted his quiet thanks for hosting the reception. Instead of going into the parlor to wait, he volunteered to greet their guests with her, freeing Alice to help Jane bring the last of the buffet platters from the kitchen. Ethel checked to be sure the answering machine was on, and then announced she was going into the parlor to watch over Lloyd and her tarts.

"Don't you trust me with them?" the mayor teased.

"I counted before we came over, and there were two missing," Ethel said, slapping him lightly on the arm. "You're as bad as Daniel was."

"Your aunt is a very interesting person," Kenneth commented after Ethel led her beau away. "She was very close to your father, wasn't she?"

"Yes, she was. She moved here after her husband died to be closer to him and us girls." Through the front window, Louise spotted two cars pulling up the drive. "I should mention, Pastor, that my aunt has not quite accepted the idea that you will be the head minister now."

"These things always take some time, for everyone." When she looked at him, worried that he might have heard about Ethel's negative opinion, he only smiled. "I have to get used to the idea, too."

A half-hour later, they finished greeting the last of the guests, among whom were several members of other churches in the area. Kenneth accompanied Louise into the parlor, where everyone was admiring Jane's wonderful buffet. The low voices hushed when the rest of the guests saw Kenneth and Louise come in.

"Thank you all for coming," Louise said, drawing Kenneth to the front of the room. "We've come here today to

welcome Rev. Kenneth Thompson as the new head pastor of
Grace Chapel. As you may know, Pastor Thompson hails
from Boston, which means we should probably convince him
to make the baked beans for our next church picnic."
Everyone chuckled at that. "Pastor, would you mind saying a
few words to get things started?"

"Thank you, Louise." Kenneth turned to address the
guests. "I'm very happy to be here with you today, and I'm
honored to have been chosen to serve God and the community of Acorn Hill. In the years since I became a parish minister, I have discovered the joys of having a strong spiritual
life, but I have always yearned for a simple place in which to
live it. City life, as you can imagine, can be very exciting and
fast-paced. And yet, no matter how many people you meet, it
is difficult to feel at home in a city. From the first time I visited this town, I knew it was exactly what I'd been looking
for—where I wanted to live, where I wanted my home to be.
I am very grateful for the chance you've given me to be able
to say that. Would you all join me in a short prayer?"

As all bowed their heads, the new minister continued.
"Lord, You are our light and our salvation. We thank You for
the many gifts which You have bestowed upon us. We look
forward to sharing our lives with You and each other through
worship, fellowship, learning, and service. Guide all of us to
be faithful and to do Your work, here and always, through the
blessings of Christ our Lord. Amen."

He paused to look at some of the faces around him
before adding, "I also hope you will share your many blessings and experiences with me. Since I've always lived in the
city, I do have quite a bit to learn about small-town life. I
must say, I'm delighted with what I've seen so far." He
glanced at Louise. "And I'd be happy to make the baked
beans for the next church picnic—so long as someone gives
me directions on how to get there."

"That reminds me, Pastor," Fred Humbert said as he

reached into the pocket of his tweed jacket and retrieved a folded paper. "I found that map of Acorn Hill you were looking for." He handed it to Kenneth. "Now while you're out and about, you won't end up driving to Pittsburgh by accident."

A few nervous laughs went around the room, but everyone still looked a little uneasy. Despite the joke about the baked beans, Kenneth's short speech and opening prayer had been much more serious than Daniel's would have had been at such an event. That only drew more attention to how different the new minister was.

"Louise, I'll get everyone started on the refreshments," Alice whispered to her, "and maybe you could play something?"

Kenneth overheard them. "I haven't had the pleasure of hearing you play yet, Louise," he said. "Would you mind taking a special request?"

"Not at all." She went over to the piano. "What would you like me to play for you, Pastor?"

"It's been a long time since I heard my favorite hymn, 'Amazing Grace.'" He looked around the room, then smiled. "There you are, Henry. Would you mind singing accompaniment with Mrs. Smith?"

Alice was standing next to Henry and Patsy Ley when Rev. Thompson made his startling request, and actually choked when she heard the words and spent several moments coughing.

Patsy handed her a napkin. "Alice, can I get you some water?"

Pastor Thompson came over to them. "Everything all right?"

Didn't Patsy hear him ask Henry to sing? And how could he ask him to do it? She felt sure Kenneth would have noticed Henry's stutter when he had introduced Bruce Golding before that candidate's disastrous sermon two weeks earlier. "I'm fine," she gasped.

"As long as you're sure." Patsy didn't seem to be upset at all.

"Pastor." Alice met his gaze and tried to choose her words carefully, so as not to embarrass either Henry or Patsy. "I think it would be better if Louise plays the song by herself."

Kenneth looked at his associate minister. "You don't mind accompanying Mrs. Smith, do you, Henry?"

The associate minister flushed, but smiled shyly. "I'd b-be h-h-happy to."

Pasty smiled at both of them as if nothing was wrong.

"There, you see? Henry's perfectly willing." Without noticing the horrified stares being directed at them from the other guests, Kenneth accompanied the associate minister to the piano.

Alice cringed. Louise appeared to be as aghast as she was, her gaze moving from Kenneth to Henry and back again. There were more whispered comments around them, and many people were beginning to look upset. Henry, whose stutter was an unavoidable affliction, was part of the Acorn Hill family and held in affectionate regard by the entire community. No one wanted to see him deliberately humiliated like this.

Her aunt made a beeline for her and tugged her away from Patsy.

"Alice, we have to stop him," Ethel whispered furiously, clutching her arm. "Henry means well, but he can't do this, not in front of all these people. Not while Louise is playing."

Alice was glad her aunt had finally given appropriate acknowledgment of Henry's burden—better late than never—and steeled herself to intervene. "I'll tell him he doesn't have to do it." She went toward Henry.

By the time she drew close enough to speak to the associate pastor, however, Louise had already begun to play the opening chords. To Alice's astonishment, Henry opened his mouth and sang in a clear, mellow tenor voice.

Amazing grace! How sweet the sound,
That saved a wretch like me!
I once was lost but now am found,
Was blind but now I see.

'Twas grace that taught my heart to fear
And grace my fears relieved;
How precious did that grace appear
The hour I first believed.

As Henry continued, he followed Louise's playing without a single hesitation. His voice never wavered once, not even on words Alice had never heard him speak without stammering over.

"Good Lord in Heaven," a woman behind Alice whispered as she listened with a rapt face. "I had no idea Pastor Ley could sing like this. No idea at all."

Neither had anyone else in the room it seemed to Alice as she looked around. All the guests were so still that they resembled garden statues. Kenneth, on the other hand, was smiling as if he had known all along about Henry's fine singing voice.

Which he must have, Alice realized. But how had the new minister discovered his associate minister's hidden talent when no one else in town had known about it?

⌒⌒

Louise had never been so hard-pressed to play the piano in her life. All she wanted to do was remove her hands from the keys and listen to Henry Ley's brilliant voice. It was only because of her years of intense self-discipline at the instrument that she was able to follow him faithfully.

As Henry sang the last line, and she played the final chords, she saw Kenneth smiling at them. The new minister's smile seemed contagious, for when the last note faded, everyone in the room was smiling. Then there was a wave of clapping, as loud and enthusiastic as from any other audience Louise had ever played before.

"T-thank you, L-Louise." Henry was a little red-faced, but he was also smiling.

She took his hand as he helped her up from the bench, then took a bow with him as the generous applause continued. "I think," she murmured, "that you could wave a feather around and knock over everyone in this room right now. That was superb, Pastor."

"Henry Ley!" Ethel came up to them, staring at the associate pastor as if he had sprouted wings. "Where on earth have you been hiding that singing voice all these years?"

"M-mostly in the s-s-sanctuary," he said, giving her a mysterious wink before putting his arm around his delighted wife.

"You should hear him in the shower," Patsy said, giving Henry a kiss on the cheek. "You'd think there was a concert going on in there."

Louise suppressed a sigh as her aunt turned on the new minister, still looking extremely suspicious. "Pastor Thompson, how did you know that Henry could sing like this?"

"I stumbled onto his secret quite by accident, Mrs. Buckley." Kenneth related how he had encountered Henry singing under his breath when he was working one afternoon. "I remembered reading about studies showing that those who stutter are often able to sing without difficulty. After I had heard Henry's remarkable vocalizing, I convinced him that he should try performing in front of the congregation." To Louise, he added, "I hope you don't mind, but I thought this reception would be a fine opportunity."

"I think it was a marvelous surprise for us all," Louise said, feeling slightly ashamed of herself for the times she had become impatient with Henry's faltering voice. "Now I cannot wait to see what kind of baked beans you make, Pastor."

That made everyone laugh, and dispelled the last of the tension in the room. Jane invited everyone to the buffet, and brought around trays of tea. Her strawberry popovers were an instant success, as were Ethel's peach tarts. While Kenneth circulated around the room, several people came to talk to Henry about his surprising hidden talent.

The reception ended on a much warmer note than it had begun, with several people asking Rev. Thompson before they left to join them for dinner or to stop by their places of business.

"The minister certainly shook up everyone today," Alice said to Louise as they waved good-bye to the last of their guests as they drove away. "I wonder what other revelations he has in store for us."

"I think it went very well." Louise felt relieved and happy. At last, it seemed there was some hope for the new pastor of Grace Chapel.

"I do, too." Jane put an arm around each of her sisters. "Now, who wants a peach tart?"

Alice frowned. "I didn't think there were any left."

"Oh, I think a couple were left in the kitchen . . . by accident." Jane grinned. "Wouldn't want them to go to waste now, would you?"

Chapter ✦ Eight

Louise had always enjoyed good health, so, outside of her annual check-ups, she seldom had to see her doctor in Philadelphia. Although she had transferred her medical records when she moved back to Acorn Hill, this was her first appointment to see her new doctor.

John Talbot was a tall, robust man who had been a general practitioner in Potterston for many years, and his friendly manner helped to put her at ease. He took the time to discuss her concerns in his office first, and made several notes as she described the unusual events at the inn and her fears that she might be responsible for them.

"I'm glad you came in to see me," he said after she had finished relating the details. "I'd like to give you a complete physical, and take some blood samples for testing. If you have a physical problem causing any memory lapses, we'll find it."

"If there is, can it be treated?"

"That depends on the type of problem." He grew serious. "We have several excellent drugs on the market now that can slow down some of the symptoms of many brain diseases like Alzheimer's. The important thing now is to identify the problem."

After her physical exam, one of the doctor's assistants

took the necessary blood samples. Louise then made an appointment to see the doctor the following week.

"Louise, you're in excellent health for a woman your age," Dr. Talbot told her as she checked out at the front desk. "Your heart rate, blood pressure and weight are exactly where they should be."

But what about my mind? "That is reassuring."

"Yes, it is," he said, and smiled. "You're in better shape than some of my patients who are half your age. Now, I want you to go home, relax and try not to worry about this. I'll see you next week to discuss your test results."

"Thank you, doctor."

After her appointment, Louise took a long walk through one of Potterston's parks to clear her head before making the drive back home. Both Alice and Jane had offered to come with her to the appointment, but she was glad she had come alone. She was not sure she could have put on a confident front for their benefit.

As the town's children were still in school at that hour, the small park was deserted, and only the sound of the breeze rustling through the leaves accompanied her as she followed the footpath down to a small, picturesque pond. There she sat down on one of the wooden benches, and watched as a pair of white ducks serenely floated by on the rippling water.

At least you have each other, Louise thought as she watched them. *I have to go through this alone. As I do every-thing else.*

There were times when she missed Eliot so much that she thought she would shrivel up inside from the pain of it, but she had never felt it more keenly than she did now. Eliot would have known exactly what to say, and he wouldn't have dismissed her fears; he would have helped her bear them.

What if I get worse? What if Jane and Alice or Cynthia have to start taking care of me? The image of Trent Alcott and his mother popped into her head. She suspected the estate buyer was obligated to bring his mother along with him; she seemed to be so frail and often muddled. Louise imagined herself becoming like Nancy Alcott and felt sick. She had always been a very self-sufficient woman, and the thought of being so dependent on others was utterly abhorrent to her.

Oh, Lord, how am I to cope with this? She rested her cheek against her hand, then remembered the unexpected kiss her youngest sister had given her there a few days before.

Jane's voice laughed inside her mind. *It's just because I love you, silly.*

She looked up and saw that another duck had waddled down to the pond and joined the pair already in the water. The trio swam over to a clump of reeds and began rooting for minnows and bugs, squawking to each other as they did.

She glanced up at the sky. *Is this Your way of reminding me that I don't have to be alone in this, Lord? That I can share this burden with the ones I love?*

Slowly Louise rose to her feet and started back toward her car.

Although Kenneth Thompson was staying at Grace Chapel Inn until the rectory was ready for him to move into, over the next week the Howard sisters didn't see much of the new minister. Like them, he rose early every morning, but after a light breakfast he left Grace Chapel Inn and usually didn't return until well after dark.

Jane found out why one breezy day when Fred Humbert stopped by to drop off some of their father's belongings.

"Afternoon, Jane." Fred walked up to the porch, carrying a large cardboard box. "I found these old papers in a closet at the rectory, and saw they have Pastor Daniel's handwriting on them. I thought you and your sisters might want to go through them and see if there's anything you'd like to save." He carefully set it to one side.

"That's really sweet of you, Fred, thank you." Jane got up from her favorite rocking chair and gestured to a pitcher of tea. "Sit down for a minute and let me fix you a cold drink—it's a hot one today, isn't it? Even with this breeze."

"That it is." He took out a handkerchief and mopped his brow before accepting the glass of iced tea. "Thank you." After he took a sip, he sighed. "That sure hits the spot. We've been so busy we haven't stopped for lunch all week."

"I could bring some drinks and sandwiches over to the rectory whenever you'd like," Jane offered on impulse. "It wouldn't be any trouble—things have been slow here at the inn this week."

"That would be real kind of you. I know the men would all chip in to cover the expense."

"If they want to, that's fine. Won't cost much with me making it." She sat down again. "What's all the rush with work about?"

"Bad weather's coming." Fred eyed the horizon as if a hurricane lurked just beyond the western hills. The breeze was rising, rustling tree branches along with their leaves, but the sky was a deep blue with only a few small stray white clouds here and there. "I've been hurrying them along to get finished before it gets here."

Jane knew one of Fred's passions was predicting the weather, but like most people she did not take him too seriously. "How bad?"

"Big thunderstorm with lots of rain. When it gets this hot and this windy so early in the year, it always means a whopper is on the way."

"Good thing we already had you repair all these old windows at the inn," she said, humoring him with a twinkle in her eye. "I can't see handing out mops and buckets to the guests when the whopper hits."

"I don't know." He shook his head and peered at the horizon again. "You might want to keep some handy, just in case."

"Will do." She noticed he was still wearing his tool belt, and that there was a trace of sawdust on the toes of his work boots. "How much more work do you have left to do?"

"We're about halfway there. This week we're replacing the bathroom tile and some rusted-out pipes in the kitchen. The church board approved my hiring some extra hands, so that's a big help."

"I didn't realize it was going to be such a major project," Jane said.

"Well, remember now that old rectory hasn't been lived in for a good many years. Pastor Daniel had this house, of course, so when he took over for the old pastor before him, he turned over the rectory to the church committees to be used for storage." Fred shook his head. "Over the years, folks have been putting everything they didn't want to throw away in there."

"Ah." She nodded. "With such a convenient place for storage, that would probably be anything that didn't move."

"And then some. We've cleared out decades' worth of old records and ledgers, books, hymnals and choir robes." He nodded at the box. "It's best you go through that out in the yard first. I found mice in the fireplace, and they made a nest for themselves there by shredding up some old robes."

"*Ugh.*" She shuddered. Next to garden slugs, mice were her least favorite critters. "Why do people save all that stuff anyway?"

"I suspect they believe in the day-after rule."

She glanced at him. "I don't think I've ever heard that one."

"You never need anything until the day *after* you throw it in the trash." He smiled and finished his glass of tea. "If I do find anything else of your father's, either I'll bring it over or send it along with the pastor."

"You mean Pastor Thompson?"

"Yes, ma'am. He's been at the rectory every afternoon,

helping us with the work." Fred got to his feet. "You know, Pastor Thompson's got a real knack for carpentry. He may dress fancy most of the time, but when there's work to do, he isn't afraid to roll up his sleeves and get his hands dirty."

That was high praise, coming from Fred. Jane thought of how much lighter in heart she'd felt since talking to Kenneth about her guilt for staying away from Acorn Hill for so many years. "I think he's going to surprise everyone."

Fred grinned. "After hearing Henry Ley sing, I'll have to agree with that."

"Hello, Fred, Jane." Ethel walked up the porch steps, clutching her straw hat as the wind tried to steal it. "Goodness, are we due for a tornado?" she asked with a mischievous smile directed toward Jane.

"Never had one hit Acorn Hill yet. I think the good Lord re-routes them for us. Thank you again for the tea. Afternoon, Ethel." Fred walked down to his pickup and drove off toward town.

"What's this?" Ethel asked as Jane put their glasses back on the tray to take it back inside. She was looking at the box Fred left on the porch.

"Some of Father's papers that Fred brought from the old rectory. Would you mind taking this tray, Aunt Ethel? I'll carry the box, it's heavier."

They brought everything inside, but recalling what Fred had told her about mice, Jane took the box back out through the side door to the garden shed, where she had a worktable.

Ethel followed her. "Why are you bringing that out here, dear?"

"I want to make sure there aren't any uninvited visitors in it before I put it in the house." Jane explained about the mice as she handed her aunt a pair of garden gloves before she donned a pair herself. "I wonder what Father could have been keeping at the rectory. I thought he had all his papers here at the house."

"It's probably some old records and such from the church office." Ethel cautiously opened one side of the top. "What else were you and Fred talking about? I thought I heard you say something about a surprise."

"Why, we're planning your next birthday party," Jane teased as she opened the other flap and peered inside. "Doesn't look like anything but old papers. I'm going to turn it over on the table."

Ethel stepped back as Jane up-ended the box and carefully lifted it. The papers were old and yellowed, and they scattered a little dust on the table, but otherwise they were free of any pests.

"This is Father's handwriting," Jane said as she stripped off her gloves and picked up some of the sheets. "It looks like a list of names."

Her aunt moved closer to peer over her shoulder. "Anyone we know?"

"I think so. 'There were more than forty disciples and prophets involved in writing the Bible, and they came from many different backgrounds. Moses was trained in Egyptian universities, and yet Peter was a fisherman. Daniel served as a prime minister in Babylon, while Luke was a physician,'" Jane read out loud.

"It was typical for your father to struggle with his studies and preparations," her aunt said in a fond voice. "He wanted people to know more about what made the Bible a unique work." She waved her hand in front of her nose, and then sneezed lightly.

"God bless you." Jane scanned the page, which provided information about the Bible through very specific details, all of it written in a tone that seemed completely unlike that found in her father's natural gift for storytelling. "This seems so different from the sermons I remember him giving, more like something a college professor would write."

Ethel opened her purse to search for something, and

gave a little chuckle. "Your mother told me that he used to worry that he wasn't scholarly enough for the congregation."

She set aside the page. "Father, *worried*? That doesn't seem possible. He always seemed so confident and relaxed when he spoke at church."

"By the time you were old enough to hear his sermons, dear, he was." Her aunt barely retrieved a lace hankie from her purse before she sneezed again. "Oh, all this dust is going to aggravate my allergies. Do you need me to help with anything else?"

"No, Aunt. You go on back in to the house." Jane began putting back the papers in the box. She was beginning to understand Ethel's attitude toward the new minister, and she suspected it had even more to do with Daniel Howard than any of them had already suspected. Still, she did not say anything as her aunt slipped out of the garden shed.

I need to talk to Alice and Louise about this, she thought as she finished repacking the box. *They might be able to recall what I was too young to remember.*

The old rectory was situated on Acorn Avenue, right next to the dry cleaners and Sylvia's Buttons. There was a path leading from Grace Chapel to the back of the rectory, and that was where Jane found Fred and his crew hard at work on the repairs.

The site was humming with activity. One of the men was sealing the framework around the exterior windows with clear caulking, while Fred and two others were unloading boxes of white bathroom tile from the back of Fred's pickup. Another man was hammering replacement shingles on the rectory's roof.

"Hello, Jane." Fred set down the box he was carrying and came over to help with her heavy picnic items. "Thank you again for doing this."

"No problem at all, Fred." Jane smiled and nodded to the other workmen as she carried a cooler of sandwiches into the rectory.

The main living room had been cleared of clutter, and the walls bore patches of gray primer in preparation for painting, but the interior still smelled rather musty. Jane noticed a makeshift worktable Fred had constructed from a sheet of plywood and two saw horses, but she saw no other furnishings.

"I made ham-salad sandwiches and some chicken sandwiches, too. And there's sweet iced tea and lemonade in the jugs," she told him as she set out the food, plates and napkins so the men could help themselves. "I also put some watermelon and pineapple slices on ice in the bottom of the cooler."

As the men took a break for lunch, Fred showed Jane their progress with the work. He had already installed new fixtures in the bathroom, and the three bedrooms were freshly painted. But all the other rooms were empty of furnishings, and when Jane asked about that, Fred grimaced.

"What was here belonged to the old pastor," he said, referring to Daniel Howard's predecessor. "The mice got to the mattresses and cushions, and the rest was either broken or dry-rotted. I hauled it all out to the landfill. It's a shame, because I know Pastor Thompson doesn't have much in the way of furniture himself."

Jane thought for a minute. "We put away a bunch of things when we were renovating the inn, remember? It's all in good shape, but I don't think we'll be using it any time soon. Let me talk to my sisters. I'm sure they'll be happy to donate some things for Pastor Thompson."

"I'd be happy to take it down from the attic and bring it over here," Fred offered. "Just let me know and I'll bring a couple of men over with me to the inn."

Jane nodded. "I'll ask them about it when I get back."

When she returned to the inn, Jane found Louise and Alice going over the monthly budget in the study, and told them about the furniture problem at the rectory.

"I don't see why we cannot donate some of the spare pieces we have," Louise said. "It's not as if we are going to be using them, and that will spare the new minister the expense of having to buy things new."

"Why don't we go up to the attic now and decide what to send over?" Alice proposed. "That way Fred can come and pick it up whenever he likes."

The three sisters adjourned to the attic, which was packed with all kinds of boxes, furniture and family heirlooms. The dust made Jane sneeze, which reminded her of the conversation she had had with their aunt in the garden shed the day before. This was a good time to discuss with her sisters her father's early days as a minister.

"Last night I looked through the box Fred brought over from the rectory," she told Alice as she tugged a sheet from a set of armchairs. "From the notes, it looked like Father worked really hard on his sermons when he first started at Grace Chapel. Do you recall anything about his ministry around that time?"

"Only very vaguely," her sister replied as she helped Louise move an old crib to one side. "I remember him spending more time at church during the week when Mother was alive, and he used to work for a couple of hours in his study after dinner. Whenever I went in to see him, he was always busy writing or reading something from a book."

"He devoted more time to writing out his sermons in those days," Louise said as she uncovered a small settee that matched the armchairs Jane was inspecting. "He even drove down to St. Joseph's University in Philadelphia a few times. I remember because Mother, Alice and I would go along with him. We would have a picnic under the trees outside the university library while he was doing his research inside."

Jane couldn't help the laugh. "I'm sorry, I just can't see Father stuck in a library surrounded by books and looking up things for his sermons. When I was little I thought he went to church to tell everyone else stories, like the ones he told us. I never thought of what he did as preaching."

"I was fairly young at the time myself, but I would say it didn't take him long to realize that what he wanted to say he could not find in a book." Louise removed a dust cloth from an old armchair and inspected the tapestry cushions. "Even back then, he loved to talk and to listen to people, didn't he, Alice? I believe that is where he picked up his style of speaking—as though he was having conversation with people, instead of lecturing them."

Alice smiled as she unearthed a small side table. "So it was really the people in this town who taught him how to give a sermon."

"I suppose they did," Louise agreed.

"That explains a lot." Jane fitted a shade to an old lamp and checked the cord. "Particularly why Aunt Ethel is—as I believe we all recognize—so reluctant to accept the new minister."

Louise folded the dust cloth and set it aside. "What does it have to do with Aunt Ethel?"

"Pastor Thompson is a very well-educated man, and an accomplished speaker." She brushed a cobweb from the edge of the shade. "He's nothing like Father was, and in a way, he's everything Father wasn't."

Alice's smile faded. "He's different, but he's not a better minister than our father was."

"No, Alice, that's not what she means." Louise opened a cabinet and peered inside. "Jane, do you think Aunt Ethel resents the new minister because he's more confident than Father was when he started?"

"Not only more confident, but more capable of meeting those challenges that being a pastor presents. Think about it," Jane said. "Pastor Thompson has handled every situation without a hitch—a disrupted Sunday service, a screaming baby, Alice's ANGELs group, the reception here, and even Henry Ley's stutter. It's only natural that she'd feel some resentment. She remembers everything Father went through when he first came to Grace Chapel. Then she sees that Pastor Thompson seems to be handling his new position so smoothly."

"By all appearances, Pastor Thompson is not having *any* problems." Louise nodded slowly.

"*Uh-huh.*" Jane spun the lamp shade, making it twirl. "You've heard her saying how he's too slick for Acorn Hill. Compared to who else but her own brother?"

"If what you say is true, then she's probably not even aware she's making these comparisons," Alice said slowly. "Should we speak to her about it?"

"No, indeed." Louise gave Alice a direct look. "You know how sensitive she is about Father. That would only hurt her feelings."

Jane went over to open the attic window to let some cooler air in. "If Pastor Thompson wasn't quite so perfect, she'd probably come around on her own. Too bad we can't get him to mess up a little." She thought for a moment. "You know, Fred told me that Kenneth has been out working at the rectory every afternoon. Maybe I'll have a little talk with him, next time I bring out lunch for the men. See what he thinks."

"I wouldn't want him to confront her about this," Alice warned. "That would only embarrass her, Jane."

Jane held up her hands. "I only want to get his opinion on what we can do. I'll make sure he doesn't mention anything about it to Aunt Ethel."

There was a faint sound of ringing from the front desk bell downstairs.

"I'll take care of it." Alice went down, then returned a few minutes later. She had an odd expression and looked a little pale. "That was Mr. Holzmann. He was looking for Mr. Alcott."

"He and his mother made reservations for the week after next, if I remember correctly," Louise told her. "Is something wrong?"

"Mr. Holzmann and his wife are going on vacation, and he asked if he could leave a check with us for Mr. Alcott. He said he'd bought some old silver from him." Alice looked out of the attic window but her gaze was unfocused, as if she were lost in thought. "The check was for a thousand dollars."

"Wow." Jane let out a low whistle, impressed. "Mr. Alcott does pretty well with what he gets at those auctions."

"He may not have gotten it from an auction." Alice rubbed her eyes before she turned to meet her sister's gaze. "After Mr. Holzmann left, I went into the parlor. Jane, all of our silver hospitality dishes are gone."

Chapter ✦ Nine

Trying to deal with the missing silver dishes and the possibility of Mr. Alcott's stealing from their inn was difficult for Alice, but she agreed with her sisters that they couldn't jump to conclusions.

"I know I have misplaced a number of things lately, and it will be a few more days before I get my test results back from the doctor," Louise said. "Let us take the time to look for the dishes first."

"I agree," Alice said, relieved. "The last thing I want to do is make false accusations."

Jane was less enthusiastic at first. "But what will we do if we can't find them? The Holzmanns will be gone for a month, and Mr. Alcott is coming back in two weeks. If he stole those dishes, he might try to take something else." She glanced at their older sister. "And another thing—I don't think there's anything wrong with you, Louise, so quit blaming yourself."

"Let us wait and see what the doctor says," was Louise's reply.

Alice felt her stomach knotting again. "Do you really think Mr. Alcott would steal from us?"

"How many times has he offered to buy something from

us?" Jane threw up her hands. "Every time he stays here, he's like a kid in a candy shop."

"We cannot blame Mr. Alcott yet," Louise insisted. "I know how suspicious this looks, Jane, but we have no direct evidence. Besides, he is an intelligent man. Why would he steal something from us and sell it to the Holzmanns right here in town?"

"You're right, that's almost like begging to get caught. Maybe it was another guest who took them." Jane rolled a hand over the back of her neck. "Like you said, Louise, we've always been so trusting of everyone."

"As we should be," Alice said. "We can't run an inn thinking everyone who comes through the door is planning to steal from us."

"No, but in the future we might consider putting away some of the more valuable antiques." Louise sighed. "Under the circumstances, I think we should go through all the rooms first and make sure we didn't misplace the silver ourselves."

They spent every spare moment that weekend looking for the missing dishes, but none of them turned up. To make matters worse, the sisters discovered that several other items around the inn had disappeared—two of Daniel's old fountain pens, the metronome Louise had used when she had been a piano student herself, and a small framed photograph of Madeleine holding Alice on her lap.

"It's like someone has gone through every single room in the house before us," Jane said at breakfast Sunday morning. "Did you two notice how many things are out of place?"

"I found some taper candles in Father's desk drawer," Alice admitted. "That seemed odd, since we've always kept them in the kitchen. And the old mantel clock was moved again, too—this time I found it on the floor underneath the piano."

"So it wasn't Charles doing that," Louise murmured absently. She caught Alice's glance. "I had Sissy Matthews and her brother for music lessons on Friday afternoon, and I kept hearing a ticking sound. I thought Charles was playing some sort of prank and ignored it."

"Maybe that's what this is, some kind of prank." Jane checked her watch. "It's almost eight o'clock. If we want to take a walk before church, we'd better get going."

As Alice changed in her room, she thought about Mr. Alcott and his mother. His slightly avaricious tendencies had made it hard for her to warm up to him, but there was no denying that he was very good to his mother. He dressed and acted like a very successful man, but what if he was concealing some sort of financial troubles? Would that have made him desperate enough to steal? If only the Holzmanns hadn't left town for a whole month.

The weather had been so pleasant lately that the sisters had made a habit of taking a walk before church. As they made their way down the path from the house, a familiar figure came from the direction of the carriage house toward them.

"Wait for me, girls!" Ethel held her hand to the crown of her hat as she hurried to catch up with them. She was clutching a folded paper in her hand and waved it at them. "Have you seen the new bulletin?"

"No, Aunt Ethel." Louise frowned. "I don't believe that we have received one yet."

"You should have gotten one, Alice, you're a member of the board." Ethel took a moment to catch her breath, then held out the bulletin. "It's all right here—he's doing exactly what I said he would. I'll tell you girls right now, I won't sit still for this. Not for a moment."

"You mean Pastor Thompson?" Alice took the bulletin from her aunt and skimmed the first page. "I don't understand—these are the usual announcements, birthdays and prayer requests. The worship schedule hasn't changed."

"Look at the back, where the pastor's message is

printed." Ethel adjusted her hat. "It's all there in black and white." She reached out and tapped on the bulletin. "Go ahead and read it out loud so your sisters can hear."

"It says, 'A call for volunteers,'" Alice read from the back page. "'Grace Chapel needs volunteers from our congregation to work on newly established committees for spiritual development, Bible study, social groups, Sunday school classes and arts and music. Interested members can contact Pastor Kenneth Thompson at the church office any weekday from 9:00 A.M. to 2:00 P.M.'" She frowned. "I didn't know we had started any new committees."

"We haven't. He's gone and done it on his own, without consulting anyone." Ethel gestured toward the church. "He hasn't been here a month, and he's already trying to change everything we love about Grace Chapel."

"I don't think a few committees constitute *everything* we love, Aunt," Louise said dryly.

"It doesn't sound like a bad thing," Jane said. At her aunt's indignant look, she added, "Why would it be?"

"Your father established all the committees that we've ever needed a long time ago," her aunt told her. "I won't have all the work Daniel accomplished pushed aside by this man. I'm going to see him, right now, and confront him about this."

"Aunt, I think you're overreacting," Louise said. "It's natural that Pastor Thompson would want to make some changes."

"Not like this, Louise, and not without consulting with the board first. Come with me, girls, we should go and see him together before services start." She stalked down the path toward the church.

The three sisters reluctantly abandoned their walk to follow their aunt.

"I haven't seen her this upset since Father's funeral," Alice murmured in a low voice. "I wish we could calm her down before she sees him."

"She has been working herself up to this for weeks."
Louise sighed. "It is probably best to get this out in the open
now, so the new minister knows what he has to deal with."

"I don't know, Louise." Alice's heart sank. "He may
decide the job isn't for him."

Jane scowled. "Well, if anyone can drive off Pastor
Thompson, it's Aunt Ethel."

The sisters accompanied their aunt downstairs to the vesting
room, where Kenneth was meeting with the ushers about the
planned service. They only had to wait a few minutes before
the ushers left and the pastor welcomed them in.

Kenneth brought an extra chair from the adjoining room
before taking a seat behind the desk. He seemed pleased to
see them. "What can I do for you ladies today?"

"The printer sends a copy of the monthly bulletin to
each of the board members." Ethel got up and placed the
copy of the church bulletin with his message in front of him.
"I read your notice about these new church committees this
morning. You didn't consult anyone about this, Pastor
Thompson."

"No, actually I didn't." He looked over the message.
"Did I miss something?"

"My brother established church committees that are
already working on all of these tasks," Ethel said. "I've served
on the Sunday school committee myself, and I see no reason
to form new ones."

"Most churches reorganize their committees at least
once a year," Alice felt she had to put in.

"Ours are just fine," Ethel insisted. "Your father had
them organized to handle all of the congregation's needs. We
may not be like the churches in Boston, but we like the way
things are. Changing them is completely unnecessary."

As her aunt went on with her opinions, Alice noticed that

far from taking offense, Kenneth seemed very interested and was listening to her carefully. When Ethel finally came to a halt, he nodded.

"I'm glad you told me this, Mrs. Buckley," he said. "I think you have some very valid concerns, and I appreciate your bringing them to my attention."

Ethel lifted her chin. "Well, I am a board member, after all. How things run here at the church is very important to me."

"I agree with you, which is why I put the call for volunteers in the bulletin. You see, since the death of Pastor Howard, there has been a steady decrease in attendance at services and at the other activities we offer here at Grace Chapel."

"You mean a decrease as in fewer people?" Alice asked.

"I'm afraid so." He removed a folder from his desk. "According to these figures, which I will be sending to board members along with the bulletin, almost twenty-five percent of the congregation are now attending other churches in the area. Half of the members still attending here at Grace Chapel only come during holidays like Christmas and Easter."

Alice had never noticed how empty the church had been before, but she had been rather wrapped up in her own thoughts lately.

Kenneth continued reciting facts. "Three of our Sunday school classes have been canceled for lack of attendance, and nearly all of our missions—with the exception of your ANGELs and the youth group, Alice—are either in utter disarray or have been discontinued, also because of lack of participation."

Alice saw her aunt's jaw sag. It was a shock for all four women to hear the statistics. Alice was glad the youth ministry had showed that it was still going strong, but the faltering and failure of so many others did not bode well for the future.

"This is not unusual, especially when a congregation loses a much beloved minister," he said kindly. "My main goals in forming these new committees and calling for volunteers are to work together to revitalize the congregation, bring people back to church and restart many of the missions and projects that have fallen by the wayside."

"But how could this have happened?" Ethel went from indignant to distressed. "Henry has been running everything since Daniel died. He would have said something to the board."

"I believe he has," Kenneth responded gently, "on more than one occasion, Mrs. Buckley. Pastor Ley has done everything he could for Grace Chapel, and his excellent work is the reason more people haven't left," Kenneth said. "Speaking from personal experience, I can assure you that the responsibilities have been overwhelming for him. All of this"—he indicated the statistics sheets—"is far too much to expect one minister to handle by himself."

Ethel's cheeks flushed. "I never knew Henry was having any difficulties. He mentioned some things at our board meetings, but we never did anything about them. I suppose we expected him to take care of them when he had time."

"He's not the type to complain." Kenneth removed a sheet from the folder and handed it across the desk. "This is a list of the new committees I've started, Mrs. Buckley. I know what areas need attention, but I'm not familiar enough with the congregation to coordinate the volunteers. I planned to make an announcement at services today, calling for someone willing to take on that particular task to volunteer."

"You need a committees director," Louise suggested. "Someone who knows the committees and the congregation very well."

"That leaves out you and me, Louise. And Alice already has her ANGELs," Jane said, surreptitiously eyeing her aunt.

"Given your remarkable talents, I would like you and

Henry Ley to head up the new arts and music committee,"
Kenneth told Louise. He turned to Ethel. "I was thinking
that you might consider taking the job of overseeing all the
committees, Mrs. Buckley."

Ethel seemed startled all over again. "Who, me?"

"You do know the church and the congregation better
than anyone else," he said. "People will be more willing to
work with you as a result. Also, I would like to maintain the
traditions that Pastor Howard established as much as possible, and I need someone who knows them well."

Alice couldn't believe how accurately Kenneth had read
her aunt. He was saying exactly the right things to her, as was
proved by Ethel's next words.

"Well, Daniel did talk to me a great deal about his work,
and what he had hoped to accomplish." Ethel got a faraway
look in her eyes. "He was so proud of this church and what
we were able to do for our community."

"Would you be willing to take on the extra work?" he
asked her. "I know you already have the responsibility of
serving on the church board, but I think it will tie in quite
well."

Alice still could not quite believe it when her aunt produced a tentative smile and agreed.

Kenneth stood and held out his hand. "Thank you,
Mrs. Buckley. I look forward to working with you." After he
shook her hand, he gave the sisters a rueful smile. "And now,
if you'll excuse me, I must get ready for our service."

As they made their way to the sanctuary, Ethel saw June
Carter. "Oh, there's June, I'll need to talk to her about
restarting the Sunday school committee. I'll be right back,
girls."

Alice and her sisters took their usual seats and watched
their aunt speaking with enthusiasm to the owner of the
Coffee Shop.

"I think by the end of the month," Louise said wryly, "that our new pastor will have everyone in the congregation working for him."

Jane insisted on accompanying Louise to her follow-up appointment with the doctor in Potterston, and when they arrived at Dr. Talbot's office she asked the receptionist if she could go into the office with her sister.

"Really, Jane, I'll be fine," Louise tried to insist.

"I've seen clocks that are not as tightly wound up as you are," she murmured for only Louise to hear. "Quit being so brave, you're going to make me cry."

Dr. Talbot came out to greet them and shook Jane's hand as Louise performed introductions, then led the sisters back to his office. As he sat down behind his desk and opened Louise's chart, Jane reached over and folded her hand around her sister's, which was trembling a little.

She smiled at Louise as she sent up a silent prayer. *Please, God, don't let this be bad news.*

"Well, Mrs. Smith, we have all your blood test results in," Dr. Talbot said, his voice very grave. "The lab has checked for the different disorders that we discussed during your last visit."

Jane tightened her grip.

He looked across the desk and smiled. "I'm happy to tell you that the results came back completely negative. There's absolutely no sign of any disease."

Louise reacted by letting out her breath and slumping back in her seat. "Thank the Lord."

"Amen." Jane reached over and gave her an affectionate hug. To Dr. Talbot she said, "Thanks, Doctor. Now I get to say 'I told you so' to her all the way home."

"I can always call a taxi, you know," Louise said with a shaky laugh as she drew back. "Doctor, are you sure? I'm not questioning the results, I was just wondering if there were any other tests I need to take."

"I could run a couple hundred more tests on you, Mrs. Smith, but I suspect they'd all come back negative as well. You are in superb health and you have no family history of these types of disorders. The only other option that remains open is to have psychological testing performed, but I see no indications of any emotional disorders, either. To be frank, I think it would be a complete waste of time and money."

Louise nodded. "Thank you, Doctor."

Jane tilted her head and looked at some of the photos on Dr. Talbot's desk. One showed the physician standing with an attractive woman and two teenage boys in front of a beautifully landscaped garden. "Your family?"

He beamed. "My wife and our two sons."

"Your wife keeps a beautiful garden."

"I'm afraid my wife has something of a black thumb," he said with a chuckle. "The boys and I actually tend the garden, and try to keep her out of it as much as possible."

Jane nodded thoughtfully. "You wouldn't happen to know a way to get rid of garden slugs, would you?"

"Well, I've never had a problem with them, but I recall my father always left out pie pans filled with beer. During the night, the slugs crawled into them and drowned."

Jane winced. "I don't think I can do that."

"Then you might try keeping some geese," the doctor suggested, his eyes twinkling. "They love to eat slugs, so you wouldn't have to get rid of the bodies."

After they returned to Acorn Hill from the doctor's office, Jane insisted on stopping at the Coffee Shop for a celebratory treat. "This calls for something really decadent. Something that will totally spoil our dinner."

Louise chuckled. "I get a clean bill of health, and you are already trying to make me fat?"

"Celebration calories don't count." She thought for a minute. "We need pie. Pie à la mode."

At the restaurant, Hope brought them both slices of freshly baked apple pie topped with enormous scoops of June's luscious vanilla ice cream. "You're both looking happy today, ladies."

Jane winked at her sister. "It's a gorgeous day."

"Enjoy it while it lasts." Hope poured cups of coffee for both of them. "Fred says we're due for a bad spell real soon."

One of the customers at the counter overheard her remark and chuckled. "Heck, Fred predicted we'd have four feet of snow last Christmas—said he could smell the snow coming. Then we barely got four inches."

Hope shrugged. "I don't know, sometimes that weather sense of his can be pretty accurate. Better to be safe than sorry." With a smile at Jane and Louise, she went off to greet two other customers who had just come in.

"So how do you feel, now that you know you're fit as a fiddle?" Jane asked as she dug into her pie.

"Very grateful and extremely relieved."

"I told you so." She grinned. "Sorry, I had to say it once."

"You always were a brat that way." Louise sipped her coffee. "Now my only concern is how to handle the situation with Mr. Alcott." Louise sighed. "Jane, what are we going to do?"

"Well, he and his mother will be back here in another week, so we're going to have to think of something soon." She made a face. "It's not like we can pack up all the antiques at the inn and hide them from the man."

"No, but I think we should remove some things from the guest rooms, to avoid offering any unnecessary temptation." She put down her fork. "In a way it would have been easier if this were my doing. At least then you and Alice wouldn't have to turn anyone in to the police."

Jane tried to think of an acceptable solution. If her father were alive, he would be the first person she'd ask for advice. "Maybe we should talk to Pastor Thompson about it. Remember Alice telling us how he handled that landlord in Boston? Maybe he might have an idea of what we can do."

Louise nodded. "Perhaps you are right. I will speak with him about it the next time I see him."

Chapter ⛪ Ten

The first heat wave of the year had settled in when Fred brought word that the work on the rectory was nearly complete.

"We should have it ready for the pastor to move in as soon as I see to the roof and to painting the rest of the interior," he told the three sisters. "If you ladies are ready for me to move that furniture down from your attic, I can start on Friday after work."

"You have certainly been working fast, Fred." Louise caught the worried look he was casting at the clear sky. "Still worried about storms off the horizon?"

"All the signs I've seen point to a real bad one coming," he admitted. "You can tell by watching the birds and the squirrels. They always know when something's on the way. That and the air just don't feel the same. Have you noticed how brassy it's been?"

Jane glanced out the front windows at the sky. "But we've had nothing but beautiful clear skies for weeks. Really, Fred, I think you're getting worked up over nothing."

"That's just another sign we're in for it. We should have had at least two or three little storms by now." In the kitchen

Fred put the empty cooler and picnic jugs he'd brought back from the rectory for Jane. He was also carrying a small plastic tank-type garden sprayer. "Thank you again for bringing lunch down to us, Jane. You've saved us a lot of time and aggravation."

"My pleasure, Fred."

"If you've got a minute, and a bottle of ammonia, I can show you a cure for your slug problem in the flower garden." He patted the tank he was carrying.

"You mean, household ammonia?" Jane went to the cleaning supply cabinet and returned with a white bottle. "Like this?"

"Yes, ma'am. If you'll all come outside, I'll show you the mix."

The sisters walked out with Fred through the side door, into the vegetable garden. He took the cleaner from Jane and poured a small amount into the sprayer, then filled it the rest of the way with water from the garden hose. "You need five parts water to one part ammonia. Then just spray."

Alice frowned. "Won't the ammonia hurt the plants?"

"That's why I dilute it—and you don't spray it directly on the plants, just around them," Fred told her. "The soil loves the nitrogen from the ammonia, too."

Jane grinned. "And the slugs will hate it."

"I guarantee they'll hightail it out of here." He handed her the sprayer. "Twice a week, and be sure to reapply after the big storm passes."

"When do you think it will get here, Fred?" Alice took his prognosticating a little more seriously than her sisters did. "It won't ruin our Summer Festival, I hope?"

"I think it could come on real soon, but it won't last that long. You might want to take down these trellises, and bring the lawn furniture into the shed. I can help you when I come by for the furniture you're donating to the rectory."

Louise saw the alarmed look on her younger sister's face

and quickly said, "No need to worry about that, Fred. You finish the work at the rectory, and Jane and I will take care of things here."

"I'll leave you ladies to it, then. Just holler if you need my help." With that, Fred nodded to them and walked back down the path toward the drive.

"I wonder if we really need to prepare for this storm Fred keeps talking about." Alice regarded the lush beds of flowers around them.

"I would prefer to rely on the local weather broadcast versus Fred's bad feelings," Louise said.

"My sweet pea vines have finally reached to just where I want them," Jane said, giving her sister a mock-fierce look. "So don't even *think* about touching my trellises."

"I was just concerned about that luncheon we're hosting for the new Seniors Social Circle on Friday," Alice said. "Aunt Ethel wants to have it in the garden. Your trellises are quite safe."

Kenneth Thompson came around the side of the house. "I thought I heard voices back here. Good afternoon, ladies."

"Good afternoon, Pastor." Louise smiled. "We were just discussing the possibility of bad weather."

Kenneth looked up, then frowned. "Seems like a beautiful day to me." He glanced back at Fred, who was pulling out of the drive. "Mr. Humbert making more dire predictions?"

"It's sort of his hobby," Alice said. She checked her watch. "Excuse me, I have to get ready for work." With a smile at Kenneth she went back into the house.

"Louise, I received a message about Mrs. Buckley's luncheon," Kenneth said. "Will you be seeing her today? I wanted to let her know I won't be able to attend."

"I can pass the message along when she comes for tea," Jane said. She looked up as a bell dinged inside the house. "*Oops*, that means my bran muffins are done. Excuse me, too." She hurried into the house.

"It is a never-ending hive of activity around here," Louise said with a chuckle.

"So I've noticed. I was wondering, though, if you could spare me a few minutes?" The new pastor gestured to the delicate wrought iron table and chairs in the shade of the old elm tree. "I'd like to get your opinion on something."

"Certainly." Louise had been so busy she had not taken a break all day, and she had been thinking about consulting Kenneth on the situation with the missing items at the inn. "Aunt Ethel has not been stirring up more trouble for you, I hope," she said as they walked to the shady spot and sat down.

"On the contrary—your aunt has been extremely helpful. She was the perfect choice to oversee the new committees, because she does know everyone and everything that goes on in Acorn Hill." Kenneth sat up to remove his jacket, then draped it over the arm of the chair. "I'm not avoiding her luncheon, by the way—I have a prior commitment. Every Friday I've been trying to visit patients at the hospital over in Potterston, and I promised one couple that I would definitely be there this week." He told her a little about the husband, who was suffering from a terminal illness.

"Alice mentioned that she had seen you at work," Louise said. "My father used to make regular weekly visits, too. He always thought that prayer was as important as any medicine."

"It can be immensely helpful to patients and their families." He studied her face. "Do you feel the same way?"

"I believe that people who are sick and suffering can take a great deal of comfort from prayer."

"I'm glad you feel that way," he said, "because I was hoping to convince you to come and visit some patients with me this Friday."

Louise hadn't expected that request, and became guarded. "Why would you need me to come along?"

"I still have a lot to learn about Acorn Hill, particularly

the names to go along with the faces," he explained. "You could help me in that respect. I think some of the patients would feel more relaxed seeing a familiar face with me, too."

Louise had an instant, terrible urge to refuse the minister's request. The hospital had never been her favorite place to begin with, and she hadn't spent any time in one since her husband's death. Even when she had gone with Jane to check on Mrs. Golding, simply waiting for Alice in the lobby had made her skin crawl.

But what if Cynthia, or Jane, or Alice became ill? What if they ended up in the hospital? Would her fear keep her from comforting her daughter and sisters?

"I don't know, Pastor," she finally said. "Alice actually might be more helpful in this situation."

"I did ask your sister, but she told me she would be busy helping your aunt and Jane with the luncheon."

That was true—and Louise had no students or other commitments that day. *It is not like I am going into the hospital*, she told herself. *After what I went through, taking those tests, this should be easy.* "If you're sure that you want me to accompany you, then I will."

Louise regretted those words as soon as she stepped out of the hospital elevator with Pastor Thompson the following Friday and saw the sign pointing to the oncology ward. Kenneth had told her the husband of the couple he had promised to visit was struggling with a terminal illness; she might have guessed it would be cancer.

She hated cancer. It had taken Eliot from her, and now it was stealing someone else's husband. The poor woman . . . Louise knew exactly what she would face in the weeks ahead. Every moment she had spent in the hospital, waiting at Eliot's bedside for a miracle that had never happened, was permanently imprinted in her memory.

I do not want to be here, she thought. *I do not want to see this happening to someone else.*

Kenneth noticed her hesitancy as they drew near the double doors leading to the ward. "Louise?" He took her arm. "Are you having some second thoughts about this?"

She was slightly embarrassed; obviously he could see how afraid she was. "At the moment, I'm feeling a little light-headed," she said, quite truthfully.

"Here." He guided her to an empty family waiting room adjacent to the ward. "May I bring you something? A cup of coffee, or a cold drink?"

He is acting so alarmed, Louise thought. *I must look dreadful.* She forced her voice to remain steady as she replied, "No, Pastor, thank you."

He bent to take her hands in his, and his eyes widened. "Your hands are freezing. Let me take you home. I can come back later."

"Please, that's not necessary. I think if I just sit and rest awhile here, I'll be fine." She felt ashamed of what she regarded to be her cowardice, and gestured abruptly toward the door. "You go ahead, and I will catch up with you in a few minutes."

"You're sure?" When she nodded, he straightened and released her hands. "All right, but you stay here and rest. I don't want to add your name to my visits list."

As soon as he left, Louise sank back in the chair and closed her eyes. She had come here to battle the last of her fears, and instead ended up acting like a foolish old woman. *I am an old woman,* part of her insisted. *I am old and I should not be putting myself through this. It is like trying to play the Saint-Saëns "Carnaval" by myself.*

The "Carnaval 14 Finale," composed by Camille Saint-Saëns, was a duet for piano that she hadn't thought about since Eliot had died. It had been the most difficult composition she had ever attempted to play in duet with her husband. They had practiced together for weeks, picking their way through the deceptively simple-looking chords and movements, literally working their way up to the furious *molto allegro* speed of the piece.

The first time they successfully played the piece without a single mistake, Eliot had brought out a bottle of champagne and insisted on a toast. "To you and me, my darling— nothing can beat us, not even that clever Frenchman's insane composition."

With their love of music and devotion to each other, they had shared so many moments like that. It was why Eliot's illness had come as such a shock—life was a duet, and she could not play it by herself.

Even as careful as she had been to conceal her feelings about his illness and subsequent rapid decline, her husband had known.

"I won't be here for all of the music you will play," Eliot had told her, his thin hand holding hers. "But I will be waiting in the wings for you, Louise, and I will be listening."

She had wept then, all the bitter tears she had been holding back. "How will I go on without you?"

"Death isn't the end of love, my dear. It's only the intermission," her husband had murmured just before he drifted off to sleep.

That was the last thing he had said to her. Eliot never awakened, and he died three days later, leaving the world as gently and peacefully as he had lived in it.

"Louise?" A woman with heavily silvered dark hair appeared in the doorway. There were deep shadows under her eyes, and she looked tired, but she smiled happily at her. "Don't you recognize me?"

Even with the familiar smile and voice, it still took Louise a moment to recognize one of her best friends from high school. "Dorrie?" The last time she had seen Dorothy Kerchner, she had been a vivacious brunette, and at least fifty pounds heavier.

"Older and quite a bit thinner and grayer, but yes, it's me," she said as she came in and gave Louise an affectionate hug. "It's lovely to see you, my dear, but what are you doing here?"

"I came to do some visiting," she said, stunned at her friend's frailty. "You are not a patient, are you?"

"Oh, no. My husband is." Dorothy's smile wobbled for a moment before she pinned it back into place. "Bernard was diagnosed with colon cancer last year." Before Louise could say anything, Dorothy shook her head. "There's nothing to worry about. He's had the last of his chemotherapy treatments, and he's going to be just fine."

Louise thought she saw tears glinting in her friend's eyes. "I wish I had known, I would have called or come to see him. I am so sorry, Dorrie."

"Thank you, Louise, but we'll get through this. You know Bernie—he's got the constitution of a bear and the appetite to go with it." Dorothy glanced over her shoulder. "I'm just going in to see him. Would you have time to stop in now? I know he'd love to see you."

Louise didn't even hesitate. "Of course I will."

She walked with her friend to the oncology ward and down the long corridor to Bernard's room. Inside, Louise was startled to see Kenneth Thompson sitting beside the hospital bed, reading from the Bible.

"'May your unfailing love be my comfort, according to your promise to your servant. Let your compassion come to me that I may live, for your law is my delight.'" The minister paused when he saw Dorothy and Louise come in.

"Look who I found in the waiting room, Bernie," Dorothy said, the cheerful tone in her voice becoming somewhat strained.

If the changes in Dorothy's appearance were drastic, Bernard Kerchner looked like an *entirely* different person. Louise saw nothing of the energetic, fast-talking salesman he had been in the bald, painfully thin old man resting in the hospital bed.

The one thing she could be sure of was that Bernard Kerchner was not fine, not at all. Eliot had looked like this a few weeks before he had passed away.

Louise kept the shock out of her voice and expression. "Hello, Bernie. What are you doing, loafing around in here?"

"Louise, it's been ages." Pain laced his voice, but his smile was genuine. "Dorrie and I were talking about you just the other day—but I thought you were still living down in Philly."

"I moved back home to Acorn Hill last year." She went over and bent down to kiss him on the cheek. His skin felt as brittle and dry as it looked. "My sisters and I inherited our father's old house, and we decided to become innkeepers and make it into a bed and breakfast."

"Which they have done with great success," Kenneth added. "I've never stayed at a more charming place."

Louise tried not to stare at Bernie, but she kept thinking of Eliot, and her gaze was drawn back to his face. The same strange sort of resolution was in his eyes, that acceptance that came just before the end.

"I remember that lovely old house, what a wonderful idea," Dorothy said, coming to stand beside Louise. "We should stop in after you're released, Bernie. We could spend the weekend and catch up with Louise and her sisters."

Her husband's expression became a blend of sadness and pity. "You know that's not going to happen, Dorothy."

"Don't be silly." Louise's friend began straightening the linens around him. "You're going to be right as rain in no time, you'll see. You always bounce back, Bernie." She took a deep breath. "Excuse me for a minute, sweetheart."

Dorothy hurried from the room.

Kenneth rose from his chair, concerned. "Should I go with her?"

"No, thank you, Pastor. She leaves so I won't see her crying." Her husband's smile bent at the edges. "Lately she's been popping in and out of here so much I barely get two minutes with her at a time."

"If you don't mind my asking, Bernie," Louise said, "what is the outlook?"

"The doctors have done what they can, but my cancer isn't responding." He sighed, then gazed at the small window on the other side of the room.

It broke Louise's heart to see him so resigned, yet it confirmed her suspicions. "No chance of another treatment?"

Bernie shook his head.

Dorrie returned, and her face looked freshly washed. "I'm back."

"Maybe you can talk some sense into her," Bernie said. "You lost your husband to cancer, didn't you?"

Louise nodded. *My husband, and a huge part of my life.*

"Sweetheart, don't start that again." Dorothy made a low, hurt sound in her throat as she sat on the edge of the bed and took her husband's hand in hers. "You're not going to die. You've got years and years left to live."

He closed his eyes. "You can't keep doing this to yourself, Dorrie. You know what the doctors have told you, and they've been very honest. You need to face it. I am going to die."

Kenneth took Bernie's hand in his, then gazed across the bed. "Dorothy, perhaps if we pray together."

"I don't have to pray. I know there's hope." Dorothy gave Louise a wild look. "Tell him, Louise. Tell him that there's always hope."

"It is good to hope, and pray, and it is also good to face the truth," Louise said, drawing up a chair so she could sit close to the couple. "It is just hard doing all of that at the same time, isn't it?"

"I don't have to face anything." Dorothy stroked her hand over her husband's brow. "I'm not going to lose him. God wouldn't do that."

Kenneth put a hand over hers. "It's not forever, Dorothy. Jesus assured us of that when He said, 'I am the resurrection and the life. He who believes in me will live, even though he dies; and whoever lives and believes in me will never die.'"

"Pastor, my husband is a strong, healthy man," Dorothy insisted. "He always has been, all of his life. He *will* get better, I can feel it."

"What you feel is your love for him, Dorrie," Louise said quietly. "And you don't ever have to let go of that."

"That is one of God's greatest gifts," Kenneth added. "That love abides with us forever."

Tears spilled down Dorothy's hollow cheeks. "I guess you think I'm being selfish," she said to her husband.

"No, Dorrie. I will always think you're the sweetest girl in the world." With some difficulty he raised her hand to his lips and kissed the back of it. "After I'm gone, I want you to go on being the happy, loving person that you are."

Dorothy's face crumpled. "I don't want to be alone, not after spending my life with you. Oh, Bernie, we've been so happy together. Please don't leave me."

"I don't want to leave you, hon," he said softly. "But it's my time, and you have to let me go."

His words made Louise recall what her husband had told her, and how much strength she had drawn from it over the years. "Just before I lost Eliot, he told me something. He said that death isn't the end of love. It's only the intermission."

Dorothy looked at her. "Do you believe that, Louise?"

"Yes, I do." She smiled through her own tears. "With all my heart."

Louise stayed with Kenneth and the Kerchners until visiting hours were over and then insisted on taking Dorothy with them to the hospital cafeteria for a light meal.

"I know you aren't feeling hungry, but you have to keep

up your strength," she said over her friend's initial protests. "For Bernie's sake as well as your own."

In the cafeteria, Kenneth sat and listened as Louise coaxed Dorothy into telling them about her children and grandchildren, and admired the wallet photos she produced of each. Louise watched with satisfaction as a little color came back into her friend's face and the worry lines across her forehead smoothed away. By the time they said good-bye in the parking lot, Dorothy looked and sounded much better.

"I'll be back to visit in a few days." Kenneth pressed her hands between his. "In the meantime, Dorothy, remember His promise to us: 'For God so loved the world that he gave his one and only Son, that whoever believes in him shall not perish but have eternal life.'"

"I'll try, Pastor Thompson."

"Call me," Louise said, pressing a slip of paper with her phone number into her friend's hand. "Whenever you want to talk, whatever you want to talk about, just pick up the phone. I'll be there."

Dorothy gave her a shaky hug. "Thank you so much, Louise."

As Kenneth pulled out of the hospital parking area, Louise took a handkerchief from her purse and blotted the last of the tears from her eyes.

"I didn't know your husband died of cancer," he said. "No wonder you reacted the way you did. This visit must have brought back some terrible memories for you. I am so sorry, Louise."

"It is not necessary to apologize, Pastor. I do try to remember the happy times, and it was good to see my friends again." She glanced back at the hospital. "Well, no, that is not exactly true. It was difficult, seeing Bernie like that—the same way Eliot was toward the end. It was a little like going through it all over again."

She went on to tell Kenneth about her husband's cancer, and how quickly he had succumbed to it.

"I was devastated at the time," she added, "but now I think I am glad that he didn't suffer through an extended illness."

"I think Dorothy will feel the same way," he said. "Once she's had time to adjust to the loss."

"In some way, that's the worst part—the adjustment, I mean. Death can be such a swift thing. Living alone after someone you love has died can seem like one endless, silent punishment. Or like trying to play a duet by yourself." She took a steadying breath. "I felt so isolated and useless after my husband died. Sometimes it took every ounce of my strength simply to endure the emptiness of the days without him."

"I felt the same when I lost my wife. I wasn't blessed to have as many years with Catherine as you shared with Eliot, but I'll always treasure the short time we did have. Losing her taught me that no experience, however tragic, is wasted."

"I don't know, Pastor." She sighed. "Losing my husband was the worst thing that ever happened to me. It is not something you can get over easily, if ever."

"Yet what you've endured allowed you to help Dorothy face losing her husband. That's something she wouldn't do before today," he said. "She's been in complete denial about his illness. Bernard didn't ask me to visit him for his sake. He wanted me to counsel her and try to get her ready for what she'll have to deal with when he passes on."

"That explains why she was trying so hard to be cheerful, when it is obvious she hasn't been eating or sleeping well for weeks." Louise was glad she had given her old friend her phone number. "Poor Dorrie. I do know how she feels."

"You were able to reach her, when I couldn't." He smiled at her. "Dorothy listened to you, and took comfort in what you said, not only because you're her friend but because you've been where she is now." As he pulled into the drive to the inn, he added, "Bernard will be able to rest easier, and when the time comes, I think Dorothy will be able to cope better with his passing. For that, I am very grateful."

She looked up at the beautiful old house that had become her new home, and realized how truly blessed she was, in family and friends. Her life was no longer empty, or meaningless—and although part of her would always miss Eliot, she was very glad to be alive. "Thank you, Pastor."

Chapter Eleven

The next day Ethel stopped in to let her nieces know that the Seniors Social Circle had declared their luncheon a complete success. Alice and Jane were working together in the garden, pruning the lilac bushes now that the last of the florets had bloomed for the year.

"They'd like to have a standing reservation to meet here at the inn every month," Ethel told them as she watched Jane thin out a third of the older canes on one bush. "The meetings will be for fellowship, Bible study and mission discussions. Should you be cutting that back so much, dear? The poor thing is beginning to look a little reedy."

"You have to be tough on lilacs, or you don't get as many flowers next spring," Jane told her as she wrestled with one particularly thick branch. "Would you hand me those big clippers, Aunt?"

Ethel passed her the clippers. "They were also wondering if you could serve some kind of inexpensive refreshments."

"It wouldn't be any trouble to offer a light tea or brunch for them, as long as they let me know a few days before the meeting how many people will be attending." Jane finally removed the stubborn cane and tossed it onto the pile on the garden path. "You know, now that we've started taking group reservations, I should put together a separate menu for catered meetings."

"Alice, Jane?" Louise came out of the house, looking extremely worried. "Oh, Aunt Ethel, I'm glad you are here. I just watched the noon news report. The weather bureau has issued a severe weather alert and flood watch for three counties, including ours. There is a huge storm front coming directly this way."

"Dear Lord." Alice dusted off her jeans as she rose to her feet. "When is it supposed to get here?"

"They are expecting extremely high winds along with lightning and heavy rains by 6:00 P.M." Louise looked around the garden. "We have to make preparations right now."

Ethel covered her mouth with one hand. "Goodness, this is exactly what Fred has been predicting, all along."

"I'll start getting things ready inside," Louise said. "Call me if you need anything."

Jane immediately took stock of what had to be removed from the yard and gardens and stored away before the storm arrived. That included the three trellises Jane had put up over different areas along the garden path. "We can put the table and chairs in the garden shed, and those benches are heavy enough to stand the wind. Those trellises won't fit, though."

"We could take them apart," Alice suggested.

"With all the lawn furniture in the shed, they won't fit." Jane said. "We'll have to lay each piece flat on the ground, and weigh it down with some rocks." She inspected the vegetable garden. "We should bring in everything that's ripe now. The wind will likely pick the rest."

"I'd better scoot home and get my shutters closed and my potted plants inside," Ethel said. "You girls be careful!"

"Do you need any help?" Alice asked.

"No, you have enough to do here. I'll ask Lloyd to come over." Their aunt hurried off, only pausing to call back,

"Don't forget to take down those wind chimes from the porch, or they'll likely end up in New Jersey!"

Alice helped Jane until a call came in from the hospital, where she was needed to work an emergency shift. Because of the severe weather warnings, the hospital had activated its community response plan in preparation for any accident victims.

"I probably won't be home until after the storm clears, but I'll try to call and check in with you tonight," she told Louise before she left.

Wendell seemed to sense the coming storm, for he anxiously followed Jane and Louise from room to room. The skies gradually darkened as heavy black clouds rolled in from the southwest. Thunder rumbled at a distance, and flashes of lightning briefly lit up the gloomy air.

"You know, the next time Fred starts talking about the air feeling brassy and the squirrels acting crazy," Louise said as she peered out of the window, "I think I am going to listen to him."

The phone rang, making Jane start. "I hope that's not Fred, calling to say 'I told you so.'" She went to answer it while Louise watched the dark curtain of rain approaching.

A moment later, Kenneth came in, closing a black umbrella and placing it in the stand by the front door.

"It's raining so hard you can't see beyond the tree line," he said after he greeted Louise. "Henry and I were able to secure things at the church. Is there anything I can do to help you here?"

She took his damp coat and hung it on the beech rack to dry. "No, we have prepared as best we can."

At the front desk, Jane put down the phone. "Hello, Pastor. Louise, Aunt Ethel says not to worry—Lloyd will be staying with her at the carriage house until the weather clears."

Louise looked up as she heard the sound of a car pulling

up the drive. "Goodness, who would be out driving in this weather?" She looked outside to see a familiar blue sedan, then went to open the front doors as Trent Alcott and his mother hurried in.

"Hello Mrs. Smith, Ms. Howard," he greeted them, a little out of breath. "Would you have two rooms available for us?"

∽

Louise showed Trent and his mother to their rooms while Jane and Kenneth went to get the oil lamps and candles from the kitchen storage closet. Kenneth volunteered to fill the bases and test the lamps.

"Would you like to have dinner with me and Louise tonight?" Jane asked as she brought a bottle of lamp oil to the table. "I'll see if the Alcotts would like to join us, too."

"That's very kind of you to offer, but I don't want to put you to any trouble."

"Since we're a bed and breakfast, we usually don't provide dinner for our guests, but you won't be able to go out for anything in this weather." She went to inspect the contents of the refrigerator to see what she could use up.

"If you want to fix something simple, like sandwiches, that would be fine," he assured her. "I know you weren't expecting three guests for dinner on such short notice."

"I didn't expect Mr. Alcott to come back here."

Kenneth carefully replaced one fluted glass lamp top. "He and his mother are regular guests, aren't they?"

Jane was tempted to mention the incident with the check and the missing silver dishes, but she remembered the conversation with her sisters about not jumping to conclusions. "Yes, they are. I meant, to come back here in such terrible weather." She took out some soup stock she had made the day before and studied the assortment of vegetables they had picked to save from the storm.

"Inns have always provided safe haven to travelers, and yet when the Holy Family needed sanctuary, they were sent to the stables." A match flared as Kenneth lit the wick and turned it up and down. "Let us hope there will always be room here at Grace Chapel Inn for whoever needs it."

"I don't think we could ever turn anyone away." Jane put the stock on the stove to heat and began washing and chopping the vegetables. *No matter how much they deserved it*, she couldn't help adding in her mind.

"The Alcotts will be resting in their rooms until dinner," Louise said as she came in. "I invited them to join us, by the way."

Jane nodded. "I did the same with Pastor Thompson."

Lightning crashed outside, making Louise jump. "Goodness, that was close. Jane, would you mind if I make some tea?"

"Go right ahead." Jane collected the celery, onions, carrots, tomatoes and green beans she had diced, and then put them in a skillet and lightly sautéed them. "I'm making 'mystery soup.'"

Kenneth looked from the stove to Louise. "That wouldn't be in any way related to 'mystery meat,' would it?"

"Probably. My father would make it every time the power went out when we were kids." Jane grinned at her sister. "Remember how he would make us guess what he put in it?"

"He should have called it 'empty the refrigerator soup.'" Louise put on the kettle. To Kenneth, she explained, "In the old days, the power company would sometimes take a day or more to restore electricity after a storm. Since we had a gas stove, our father could always cook, so soup was a good way to use up food that might otherwise spoil."

"Hence the mystery." The new minister nodded to himself. "I doubt I will prove much of a food sleuth. My parents were more concerned that I'd just clean my plate."

Louise smiled at that as she took a mug over to Jane, who

was stirring the contents of the pot. "What will you be serving with that?"

"I thought I'd make a green salad and stuffed chicken and onion croissants, and have some of that white chocolate cake I made yesterday for dessert." Jane put the top on the stock pot and tilted her head, listening to the rain. It was falling on the roof with pounding force now, and the wind was rising. "Lord, that does not sound good at all."

"I'll set these lamps out on the front desk," Kenneth said. "Louise, would you like me to take two of them up to the Alcotts?"

"If you wouldn't mind, Pastor, that would be very helpful." As soon as he left, Louise exhaled, then touched Jane's arm. "Have you mentioned anything to him about our situation with the Alcotts?"

"No, but it was really difficult not to. I just wasn't sure if I should with them here." Jane helped her sister prepare the teapot and set out three cups. "I still can't believe they came here. What are we going to do?"

"We certainly can't ask them to leave, so we will have to make the best of it." She placed the creamer and sugar bowl on the breakfast table. "I still have the check that Joseph left for Mr. Alcott. I will have to give it to him."

"No, you won't." Jane set down the teapot, making the cups clatter in their saucers. "That check could be the only evidence we have."

"It does not belong to us, my dear, we cannot keep it."

"We could misplace it temporarily." She saw her sister's reaction and sighed. "All right, it's not exactly honest, but consider this, Louise: if that check is payment for our stolen silver, then the money doesn't belong to him, it belongs to us."

"And if it is not"—Louise rubbed her right temple—"that would make *us* the thieves."

"I'm not suggesting that we actually steal it, just let it slip behind something or get shuffled in with the tax receipts—anything that would take a long time to search through in order to find it." She heard footsteps and lowered her voice. "We have to do *something*. We might not get another opportunity like this again."

Her oldest sister looked up at the ceiling and sighed. "Honestly, Jane, I hope we never do."

The wind was howling and the lights flickering by the time Jane had dinner prepared and ready to serve.

"Let's eat in the kitchen," she suggested to Louise. "That way, if we lose the power, I won't have to carry dishes back and forth and fall on my face in the dark."

Kenneth brought a folding table in from the parlor and set it up in order to extend the breakfast table. Mr. Alcott insisted on carrying in an extra chair and setting the table with Louise. His mother hovered by the garden window, watching as the wind whipped through the trees and flowers outside.

"This is wonderfully cozy," he said, admiring the old cabinets and inspecting everything on the counters. "It reminds me so much of my mother's kitchen when I was a boy. We had a little house in Scranton with the same kind of sink."

"You never eat like you should, Trenton," his mother said, sounding a little vague. She turned from the window to ask Kenneth, "How can a boy grow up big and strong if he won't eat his vegetables?"

"My mother insists that I would be much shorter had I not eaten mine," the new minister assured her with a perfectly straight face.

"Come and sit down, Mother." Trent went over to guide her away from the window.

Mrs. Alcott seemed to snap back to the present as she sat next to her son at the table. "Everything looks so lovely."

"Pastor, would you say grace?" Louise asked.

"Of course. Let's all join hands." When everyone had done so, Kenneth bowed his head. "Dear Lord, we thank You for the gifts of Your bounty that we have before us at this table. This food, which You have already blessed in the giving, so further bless in our partaking. Give us grateful hearts for all Your mercies, make us mindful of the needs of others, and watch over those who cannot be with us tonight, through Christ our Lord. Amen."

"Thank you, Pastor." Louise smiled. "That was lovely." While she passed around the platter of croissants, Jane left the heavy soup pot on the stove and filled the bowls on the counter before bringing them to the table. The delicious smells perked up everyone's spirits.

"I've never seen this treat before, Ms. Howard," Trent said as he studied the contents of his bowl. "What do you call it? 'Everything-but-the-kitchen-sink soup'?"

"'Mystery soup,' but I like your idea better—I may steal it for our catering menu." Jane paused, met Louise's horrified gaze, and cleared her throat. "I mean, *borrow* it, Mr. Alcott."

"You really shouldn't make soup in the sink, dear." Mrs. Alcott patted her hand, and then beamed at Kenneth. "If you marry this nice young man here, I'm sure he'll buy you some pots."

This time Louise nearly choked on her soup, but Jane took the comment in stride and smiled at Kenneth. "I have all the pots I need right now, Mrs. Alcott, but I will keep the suggestion in mind."

Halfway through dinner lightning struck very close by, and the lights went out, startling everyone. Louise and Jane were prepared, however, and lit the table lamp. The diffused glow added a delightful touch of intimate warmth to the meal.

"When we met, you mentioned that you were an estate buyer, Mr. Alcott," Kenneth said to Trent. "Where do you resell what you buy?"

"Call me Trent, please. My father kept a shop in the city for years, but I prefer not being tied down to one place." He nodded toward the window. "When I'm out on the road, I buy at estate sales and ship the goods directly to my customers. I mainly sell to interior designers and antique dealers who already have shops themselves, so there's no need for me to maintain a storage space with inventory."

Kenneth nodded. "Do you know Joseph and Rachel Holzmann from Acorn Hill Antiques in town?"

Jane gave Louise a meaningful glare. Louise shook her head slightly.

"Yes, I often stop in at their shop when I'm in the area. A nice couple, and very shrewd." He picked up his fork, taking a moment to admire the heavy silver plate. "I sold them a few collectors' pieces the last time I was staying here at the inn."

Louise coughed into her napkin.

"Really." Kenneth seemed very interested. "What were they?"

Jane held her breath.

"Just some antique silver I'd picked up here and there." Trent stabbed his salad. "Mr. Holzmann gave me a good price for them, but then he's a fair man and an excellent dealer. You never know with the people you meet in this business—some of them seem pleasant enough, but many of them are always wanting something for nothing."

Louise rose abruptly and took her soup bowl to the sink.

"I want you to polish the silver before Christmas, Trent," his mother said unexpectedly. "Don't try to sneak out and play baseball with your friends, and then tell me you forgot to do it."

"No, Mother, I won't." He gave Kenneth and Jane an apologetic look. "Her mind wanders a bit these days." He glanced down. "That's an unusual ring you're wearing, Pastor—something from college?"

"No, it was my grandfather's." Kenneth touched the scrolled surface of the old signet ring. "He was a cod fisherman from Gloucester. My parents let me spend a few weeks every summer with him on his boat, and he taught me everything he knew about fishing and the sea."

Mrs. Alcott peered at him. "Why didn't you become a fisherman, young man?"

"Oh, I did, ma'am." Kenneth smiled at her. "My catch is just a little different."

The power remained off after dinner, so Louise invited everyone into the parlor and played the piano while Jane served coffee and slices of her white chocolate cake for dessert. The lights from the oil lamps dispelled most of the gloom, but the storm seemed determined to compete for attention. Thunder boomed, the wind shrieked and the rains pounded against the window panes.

Finally Louise gave up trying to overcome the cacophony. "I'd play Wagner but I don't think it would be loud enough," she said, carefully closing the lid over the piano's ivory and black keys.

Jane noticed Mrs. Alcott wasn't eating, and went to her. "Would you prefer something else, ma'am?"

"Trent will be late for his violin lessons," she said, ignoring her cake as she stared at the rain-lashed window. "His music teacher gets so upset when he's late. I should call him."

"Now, Mother, you know I haven't played the violin in thirty years." Trent put an arm around her shoulder. "Why don't we go upstairs and make you comfortable for the night?"

The old woman nodded. "As long as you call your father and tell him we'll be staying in the city for the night. You know how he worries, Trenton."

"Yes, Mom, I will." He gave everyone an apologetic smile as he led her out of the room.

"Oh, Louise." Jane sat down and released a pent-up breath. "This is not going to be easy."

"Seeing someone afflicted with Alzheimer's never is," Kenneth said, "but I have the feeling Mrs. Alcott is not who is bothering you and Louise tonight."

Jane saw the look her sister gave her. "We should tell him."

"Yes, we should. We have a slight moral dilemma, Pastor." Louise got up and closed the door before she continued. "I am sure you've noticed how Mr. Alcott admires some of the antiques we have here at the inn. He has made several offers to purchase them from us whenever he has been a guest in the past."

"Several?" Jane snorted. "More like dozens."

"I can't blame him," Kenneth said. "Personally, if you ever want to get rid of that hat rack in the front room, *I'll* be delighted to take it off your hands."

Louise smiled. "We will remember that. Our problem is that Mr. Alcott took an interest in some silver hospitality dishes that we had here in the parlor. As you might imagine, we refused to sell them to him, like everything else he's offered to buy."

"Mr. Holzmann stopped by a few days later as he was leaving town on vacation, and asked us to hold a check for Mr. Alcott," Jane said, picking up the story thread. "It was payment for some antiques he had sold to the Holzmanns, and the word *silver* was written on the memo line. After Mr. Holzmann left, Alice discovered all of our dishes in the parlor had vanished."

"Now I understand." Kenneth thought for a moment. "Have you reported the theft of the silver to the police yet?"

"No, not yet." Louise sighed. "You see, we are still not

convinced that the dishes have been stolen. I have been somewhat absentminded lately, and there is a chance that I may have put them away and forgotten where I put them."

"On the other hand, Alice and I are convinced that it's not Louise. We've searched all the rooms, and they haven't turned up. Also, the dishes aren't the only things that are missing," Jane pointed out. For Kenneth's benefit, she added, "Someone has been moving things around and putting them back in the wrong place, the way you would when you're searching for something valuable. Now things have begun to disappear. I still think we should ask Mr. Alcott about the check and what silver he sold to the Holzmanns."

Louise shook her head. "We have no proof that Mr. Alcott stole anything from us, and, with the Holzmanns in Europe for the summer, no way to confirm what they actually bought from him. Until they return, or we find new evidence, our hands are tied."

The wind wailed outside the window in mournful agreement.

"That explains why you and Jane looked so upset when I was talking to Mr. Alcott at dinner." The pastor smiled regretfully. "I had wondered about that. I can see how awkward it is for you to have them here as guests now."

"Sometimes the Lord works in mysterious ways," Louise agreed. "But even if Mr. Alcott is involved, we couldn't deny them shelter from the storm. It would not be the Christian thing to do, especially to his poor mother."

Jane felt a little ashamed of herself for having considered just such a denial. "What do you think we should do, Pastor? Should we go on pretending nothing is wrong, or should we confront him?"

"Have you given Mr. Alcott the check yet?"

"No, but we cannot keep it." Louise nodded toward the front desk. "I have it in an envelope in the cash drawer. I'm not looking forward to it, but I plan to give it to him in the morning."

"I think you should do that, Louise. Jane, can you tell me what else is missing?" He listened as she recited the list of items they had not yet found. "Is there anything that has been moved more than once?"

"That old clock up there on the mantel," Louise said. "But what does that have to do with anything?"

"I have an idea. Jane, do you have some inexpensive fountain pens and a framed picture of your mother holding a child? Louise, do you have another metronome?" When they nodded, he asked, "Would you put them in the places where the others that are missing used to be?"

Louise exchanged a glance with her sister. "Why are we replacing everything that was stolen with something else?"

"I think it's a way to find out what happened to your silver," was all Kenneth would say.

Chapter ⛪ Twelve

The storm continued through the night, but toward dawn it began to dwindle in strength. Most of the wind and thunder had moved on, and the rain had almost stopped. And the power had been restored.

Kenneth came down early to meet Jane and Louise in the kitchen. "Good morning. How did you ladies weather the storm?"

"I slept like a baby," Jane said. "Rain always does that to me."

"I usually have a bit more trouble with thunder and lightning, but I fell asleep right away myself." Louise handed him a cup of decaf. "The good news is, the roof seems to be intact, I didn't find any water spots on the floors or ceilings, and not one of the windows was broken."

"I'm glad to hear it." He set his cup on the table. "Would you both come with me for a moment? There's something you need to see."

He led them into Daniel's study and went to the desk. "This is where you put the picture last night, Jane?" He touched an empty spot on the desk.

She nodded and came around to open the drawer. "The

fountain pens are gone too. Drat, I was hoping it wasn't Mr. Alcott."

"Let me check the parlor." Louise left, and returned a minute later. "The clock was moved back to the display case, and the metronome is gone."

"But it doesn't make sense." Jane frowned. "Why would he take the same things? Why would he move the clock again? Why not steal something more valuable?"

"We need to speak to Mr. Alcott about that." Kenneth looked up as footsteps sounded on the stairs. "And I believe I hear him now."

They all went out to intercept Mr. Alcott on his way to the dining room. The estate buyer greeted them cheerfully. "Sounds like the storm blew itself out. You're all up early."

"Mr. Alcott, we need your help," the pastor said. "Does your mother have a suitcase with her?"

"Yes, I brought it in last night." Mr. Alcott looked puzzled.

"Would you mind bringing it down here? I believe it will help us solve a mystery." When, after shrugging as he displayed a look of weary resignation, the estate buyer went back upstairs, Kenneth turned to the two sisters. "Like you, Louise, I don't usually sleep well during storms. At about three o'clock last night, I heard someone walking around downstairs. I decided to come down and see who it was."

"You saw Mr. Alcott take those things?" Jane whispered, her eyes wide.

"Not exactly."

Soon Mr. Alcott was back with his mother's suitcase. "Here it is, Pastor, though I don't know how it can help with anything."

"Would you put it on the desk, Mr. Alcott? Thank you." Kenneth went over as he did. "Now if you would open it, please?"

Trent flipped up the lock on each side and raised the lid.

Inside the suitcase were some neatly folded clothes, a pair of comfortable slippers, and the missing fountain pens, picture, and metronome.

Mr. Alcott stared at the stolen items. "What are those doing in there?"

"Your mother put them in her suitcase," the new minister told him. "I believe she took them around 3:00 A.M., when she came downstairs."

Louise looked astonished. "*Mrs.* Alcott took them?"

Mr. Alcott's face turned beet red. "Ladies, I apologize to you from the bottom of my heart. I can't imagine why my mother would be stealing things from you."

"She didn't steal them, Trent," Kenneth said. "I am fairly certain that she believes they belong to her."

Now Jane was totally confused. "Why would she think that, Pastor?"

Before Kenneth could answer, Mrs. Alcott slowly made her way downstairs. She was still in her nightgown and robe, and she looked very upset.

"Trent?" she called out in an agitated voice. "Trent, someone has taken my suitcase."

"I have it, Mother." Her son met her at the foot of the stairs. "Please go back upstairs. I'll bring it to you in a minute."

But Nancy Alcott spotted the open suitcase on the desk, and brushed past him. "Why are you looking at my things? Why are you trying to take them away from me?" she demanded as she came over and took the framed photo Jane was holding. "This is the only picture I have of Veronica."

"That's not Aunt Veronica, Mother," Trent said as he joined her, and gently took the picture away from her.

"Well, I found your father's good pens," she told him, "and the metronome for your sister's piano lessons. I just have to put them away where they belong."

When she took the items out of her suitcase, Kenneth put a hand on Trent's arm. "Wait. Let her put them away."

They quietly followed Mrs. Alcott as she went into Daniel's study and walked up to the reference books. She set down the pens and the metronome so she could pull out three of the heavy books.

In the space behind the books were the missing silver dishes, neatly stacked alongside the original metronome, photo and pens that had been missing.

Seeing them made her frown for a moment, before she added the new pens and photo. "They'll be safe here," she said to her son, then replaced the books. "I'm going back to bed now." She drifted out of the room as if nothing was bothering her.

It took everyone a moment to adjust to what had just happened.

"She's hidden things before, at our house, but I didn't know she was doing it here. My mother was recently diagnosed with Alzheimer's disease." Trent looked utterly miserable as he turned to Louise and Jane. "Mrs. Smith, Ms. Howard, I am so sorry about this."

Jane released a suppressed sigh. "Poor woman! I never would have guessed she was involved in any way," she responded gently. "Not in a million years."

"It is because of the Alzheimer's, isn't it?" Louise asked. "She thinks this is her house. That is why she keeps moving things too, isn't it, Pastor?"

Kenneth nodded. "It's a common thing among patients with the disease. She's putting them back where they belong—in her house." He put a hand on Trent's shoulder. "My grandfather had Alzheimer's. You know, there are some ways to help her with this."

Louise looked at Jane, and by unspoken agreement they slipped out of the room so that the two men could talk.

In the kitchen, Jane started the coffee maker and put on the kettle. "I feel so guilty for suspecting Mr. Alcott."

"So do I, but at least now he knows the truth, and he can

help his mother." Louise looked out at the garden. "I don't think the wind did much damage," she said. "There are a couple of branches on the lawn, but the trees are still intact." She caught her breath. "Jane, come and look at the sky."

Jane went over, and when she saw the lovely arc of a wide rainbow stretching over Acorn Hill, put an arm around her sister.

"'Tis better by far at the rainbow's end,'" Louise quoted softly, "'to find not gold but the heart of a friend.'"

Jane smiled in response, and then catching sight of Alice's brown striped umbrella coming up through the garden, went to open the back door for her sister. When she saw her face, she reached out to her. "Alice, what's wrong? No one was hurt in the storm, I hope."

"No, we only had a few minor injury cases at the hospital from an accident on the interstate. I do have some bad news, though." She closed her umbrella and shook it off before coming in. "The rain made the roof on Henry and Patsy Ley's house collapse. They had to spend the night sheltering at the hospital."

"Oh, how terrible for them." Louise covered her mouth. "They are all right, though, aren't they?"

"They are, but the house is ruined. They called the owner this morning to report the damage." Alice's shoulders slumped. "It turns out that the owner doesn't have enough insurance to cover the repairs. He's going to demolish the house, and Henry and Patsy have to move out immediately."

The word spread about Henry and Patsy's disastrous experience, and the day after the storm Kenneth, Fred, and a number of other people from the congregation went over immediately to help the Leys recover what they could from the weather-damaged house. Kenneth returned that night to report that the storm had indeed wreaked utter havoc on the little house, and that the wind and rain had ruined many of their furnishings and belongings.

"Henry and Patsy will be staying with Fred and Vera temporarily," the pastor told them, "until they find a new house to rent."

Unfortunately, the sisters soon learned that finding a new home meant the Leys would have to leave Acorn Hill.

"There just aren't any appropriate properties available in Acorn Hill, to rent or buy," Fred's wife told Alice when she stopped in on the way to work to return a casserole from Jane. "Pastor Ley doesn't feel that a place in Potterston would allow him the close contact with his parishioners that he feels they deserve."

"There isn't any place closer they can stay?"

Vera shook her head. "Henry and Patsy can stay with us for a few weeks, but my girls will be home from college soon, and we won't have enough rooms to go around."

"I wish we could have them stay with us at the inn, but we're already booked up for the entire month of July." Alice felt so frustrated at being unable to help their friends.

No one else was able to offer hope for the Leys, either, and the prospect of Henry and Patsy's leaving town cast a shadow over the preparations for the Summer Festival.

"Why am I doing this to myself again?" Jane grumbled.

As she brought in a tray of dishes from the dining room, Louise heard her sister's question. She saw Jane remove a loaf of bread from the oven, using a red and black striped kitchen towel to protect her hands from the hot pan.

"What are you doing to yourself now?" she asked as she went over to the stove.

"I'm baking friendship bread for the Summer Festival contest." She carefully set the pan on a cooling rack, then groaned as the golden brown oval slowly sank in the middle.

"No, no, don't you dare! Don't do that! Stop falling this instant!"

The bread continued to deflate, until it resembled a large, rather sad-looking doughnut.

Jane made a frustrated sound and stamped her foot. "I don't believe it! That's the sixth loaf I've made this week." She tossed her towel on the counter in disgust. "I will never get this recipe right."

Louise studied the dismal results. "You could glaze it and enter it in the unusual desserts category."

Jane glared at her. "There is no unusual desserts category."

"Indeed!" She went to the old red and white cookbook and examined the recipe page. "Then perhaps you could try one of the recipes that isn't quite so time-consuming— something that would be a little easier to prepare."

"I was tempted to make the Dutch dandelion wine, but I think I might end up drinking it myself after this." Jane sighed. "Plus I threw all the dandelions in the mulcher. Who would have thought you could use weeds for something other than compost?"

Louise patted her shoulder. "I am sure you will think of something."

"No, I won't." Squaring her shoulders, she picked up the next jar of bread starter she had prepared, and regarded it the same way she would a hand grenade. "I'm a trained chef. I have worked in one of the finest restaurants in the country. I will make this bread if it's the last thing I ever bake."

Louise kept a straight face until she got to the front desk, then couldn't help chuckling as she heard Jane banging pots around. Alice, who was on the other side sorting through the mail, glanced toward the kitchen with a frown.

"The friendship bread sank again," was all Louise had to say.

Alice grimaced. "Maybe we should ask Aunt Ethel if she can help her."

"No, I think that would only make things worse. Let Jane work it out on her own." Louise nodded to the crystal vase of flowers Alice had on the desk. "Are these for one of the guest rooms?"

"No, for the desk in Father's study. I was going to take it in and dust in there after I finish the mail." Alice frowned. "Louise, have you come across that other green cameo vase? I was telling Mr. Alcott about it, and I wanted to show it to him."

"No, I haven't seen it." The phone rang. "You're busy. Why don't I do the dusting, and while I'm in there, I will look for it."

"Thanks," Alice said as she answered the call.

Louise picked up the vase of flowers and the dust rag and went to her father's study.

Trent Alcott had returned everything that his mother had hidden in her suitcase, and the sisters had found the rest of the missing items—with the exception of the cameo vase—concealed behind the books on the shelves in Daniel's study. The estate buyer had also promised to check his house when they returned to make sure that his mother had not taken anything from the inn home with her.

Louise placed the crystal vase on her father's desk, and briefly admired the tiny rainbows the sun cast through the facets before wiping down the desk and chair. She vaguely remembered seeing the two vases years before on either side of the desk lamp, and checked again in all the drawers, but found nothing.

Wendell wandered in and jumped up onto Daniel's chair, stretching his neck out to see what she was doing.

"What do you want, nosy?" she asked as she flicked the end of the cloth at him. He batted at it with his paws, then latched on and tried to bite it. "No, you cannot play with this. I need it for dusting," she said as she gently untangled it from his claws.

With a yowl Wendell leapt to the desk, bumping into the crystal vase before he bounded from there to the floor.

Louise grabbed the crystal just before it tipped over. "Pesky cat. We don't need any more broken vases, thank you."

She scanned the shelves of the study. *Now, if we missed one of Mrs. Alcott's hiding places, where might it be?* She spotted a vase-sized gap between some books on one of the higher shelves, too high for Mrs. Alcott to have reached, but just to be certain Louise pulled one of the sturdy armchairs over to climb up and have a look.

There was nothing in the space. As she tried to look behind the books, Wendell jumped on the chair, startling her into losing her balance. As the chair rocked under her feet, she yelped and grabbed the edge of the shelf.

"Louise!" Jane came in and hurried over to steady the chair, and Wendell shot off and hid under Daniel's desk. "Are you trying to break your neck?"

"No." She climbed down carefully. "But I probably would have. Thanks for grabbing the chair."

"Thanks for scaring the wits out of me." Jane glanced up at the shelf. "If you are determined to clean up there, please use the duster with the long handle."

"I will. I was just looking for that other green cameo glass vase that Father gave to Mother. You haven't seen it, have you?"

"No." Jane flung the kitchen towel she was carrying over her shoulder. "And we don't have time to look for it now— Alice got a call from the hospital, they need her to fill in for someone. We've got two guests arriving this afternoon, too."

Louise stared at the towel on Jane's shoulder. It seemed to remind her of something, but she couldn't remember what. "All right. I will take over the desk, if you will check the rooms. Just let me get Wendell out of here."

Jane nodded and moved the armchair away from the

shelves before she left. Louise bent down to coax the frightened cat from under the desk, then recalled why Jane's kitchen towel had repeatedly caught her eye. It was the exact same kind of towel she had seen wrapped around the object that Rachel Holzmann had put aside so hurriedly, when Louise had stopped by their shop to invite them to Kenneth's reception.

It has to be a coincidence. Maybe she bought hers from the same store, Louise thought. *For why on earth would Rachel Holzmann have one of our kitchen towels?*

An outbreak of summer flu in Potterston required Alice to fill in for sick nurses on several shifts, and as a result she barely had enough time one week to prepare for her ANGELs meeting. It didn't help that her ANGELs and the older children from the youth group became upset when she passed around a card for everyone to sign for the Leys.

"It isn't fair!" one boy said. "Pastor Ley shouldn't have to leave town because his roof fell in. Why can't we fix it?"

Alice tried to explain why the owner of the Ley's house had no choice except to demolish the structure.

"Then why don't we build them a new house?" a girl asked. "The Amish all get together and have barn raisings. We could have a house raising."

"Houses are very expensive to build," Alice told her. "And it would take months to build one. The Leys have nowhere to live now, so they'll need to find a home right away." She was grateful to see Kenneth come in the dining room. "Here's Pastor Thompson."

"Good evening Alice, boys and girls." He went to the front of the room. "Are we working on the play tonight?"

"We will be in just a minute," she said, getting out her Summer Festival folder. "We were discussing the sad news about Henry and Patsy's having to move out of town."

"If Pastor Ley was the head minister, he wouldn't have to leave," one of the younger boys burst out. "If you hadn't come here, he could stay and build a new house."

All of the kids looked open-mouthed at the boy, then at Kenneth.

Alice was appalled. "Bobby! Apologize to Pastor Thompson right this minute!"

"It's all right, Alice, he doesn't have to." Kenneth went over to the indignant boy, who was now hanging his head. "I know how you feel, Bobby. I like Pastor Ley, too. And you're right, if I hadn't come here, perhaps he could stay in Acorn Hill."

Hearing that made several of the children gasp.

"When terrible things happen to people we care about, it's very easy to get angry and say unkind things. It's much harder to do something positive." He picked up the Bible and sought out a particular passage. "I'd like you to read verse twenty-six out loud."

Bobby pushed his bottom lip out into a slight pout, then looked at the page. "'In your anger do not sin,'" he read slowly. "'Do not let the sun go down while you are still angry.'"

"Thank you. God knows how difficult it is to resist the temptation of sin, even when we're angry. But God expects us to try very hard not to sin out of anger." He looked down at Bobby and turned the Bible to another page. "Would you also read verse twenty-nine out loud?"

"'A patient man has great understanding, but a quick-tempered man displays folly.'" Bobby's lip lost most of its pout as he scrunched up his face. "What does 'displays folly' mean?"

"It means saying something stupid, like telling Pastor Thompson he should have never come to town," one of the older boys snapped.

"It means," Kenneth said, resting a hand on Bobby's

shoulder, "doing something that is useless, something that doesn't help the situation." He looked over at the other boy. "For example, shouting in anger at someone."

Now the other boy hung his head. "Sorry, Bobby."

"Pastor Ley doesn't want to leave Acorn Hill, but does he seem angry about it?" Kenneth asked. Several of the children chorused *no*s. "I think we should all follow his example and try to be as understanding about this situation as we can."

Bobby sniffed and rubbed his nose with the back of his hand. "I'm sorry I shouted at you, Pastor."

"It's okay." He smiled down at the boy. "Now, how are the plans for the Summer Festival coming along?"

Alice showed Kenneth the script the children had prepared for the play and the list of parts to be assigned. Henry was working with the choir for the musical accompaniment, and some of the older children from the youth group had taken charge of costuming.

"We should be finished with everything on time," she told him, "but we still haven't come up with an idea for the final scene." Alice's pager beeped, and she saw the emergency number for her ward appear on the display. "I'm sorry, kids, but I need to make a phone call to the hospital." She looked at Kenneth. "Would you mind taking over for me for a few minutes, Pastor?"

"Not at all."

Alice hurried to use the phone in the vesting room. As soon as she called the number for the ward, a disgruntled doctor got on the line.

"I noticed during my rounds that Mrs. Murphy in Room 112 has developed a rash on her face and upper torso, Ms. Howard." There was the sound of paper rustling as he flipped through the patient's chart. "I see no mention of it in the notes from your last shift."

She concentrated. "Mrs. Murphy didn't have a rash when I last saw her, sir."

"Did you list all of the medications you administered to her? This looks like an adverse drug reaction, and the charge nurse said you were in a hurry to leave yesterday."

"I always note all the medications I give our patients," she assured him.

"I hope you do, Ms. Howard, because if I find out differently I will take immediate action." The doctor slammed down the phone.

Shaken, Alice slowly replaced the receiver. Had she been in such a rush that she had actually given a patient the wrong medications? She had never made such a huge mistake before.

Slowly she walked back to the Assembly Room to see Kenneth showing Charles Matthews how to cast a line with a yardstick as a pretend fishing pole. She watched as the pastor sat back down with the children, and Charles carefully guided his "pole" back and forth, his weight shifting from side to side as he did so.

"You can't catch many fish if you just drop a line into the water, can you?" He pointed the end of the yardstick at his sister.

Sissy jumped to her feet. "No!"

"You have to have the right equipment, and you have to know how to use it," the pastor said.

Charles's face took on an earnest expression as he continued pretending to cast. "Now, can you learn where the fish are by listening to someone else talk about them?" He pointed to Bobby.

The boy grinned as he popped up. "No!"

"That's right—you've got to get out there and look for them yourself," Charles said, and grinned as he saw Alice. "And what do you do if the fish aren't biting?" He pointed his yardstick directly at Alice. "Should you give up if you don't catch anything?"

She laughed and went along with the game. "No!"

Kenneth and the children clapped their hands, and Charles took a short bow before sitting back in his chair.

The pastor rose and held up the yardstick. "And the message is just that simple, kids. To be the fishers of men that Jesus wanted us to be, we need to study the Bible and share it with others. We can't depend on others to bring people to God—*we* have to do it. That's why we have events like the Summer Festival, to get out there and tell people about what we believe. And like all good fishermen, we must learn to be patient and never give up." He glanced at Alice. "That's part of one of my old sermons, minus the props. The kids and I thought adapting the idea for the final scene of the play might work, especially if Charles casts his line out to the audience so that they can help with the answers."

"I can do it, Ms. Howard," Charles assured her. "My Dad taught me to fly fish practically before I could walk."

"Plus the rest of us will have buckets of plastic fish with Bible verses on them to give out to the people in church," Bobby chimed in. "Like prizes."

Kenneth raised his brows. "What do you think?"

Her father had never done anything like it, of course—his tendency had been more traditional in his approach to the different programs they put on. But in her heart Alice knew Daniel would have loved it—it was fresh and innovative, and it brought the message across loud and clear.

"I think it's a terrific idea for the final scene," Alice agreed, then winked at the children. "As long as we don't use real fish—or real hooks."

Chapter 🪟 Thirteen

The rest of the town put out their decorations for the coming Fourth of July weekend, and the Howard sisters were busy doing the same at Grace Chapel Inn. They hung oversized bows of red, white and blue ribbon from the overhead light fixtures and raised Daniel's treasured American flag so that it fluttered gaily above the center of the porch roof.

"'You're a grand old flag, you're a high-flying flag,'" Jane cheerfully sang out of tune as she climbed down the ladder Alice held steady for her. "'And forever in peace may you wave!'"

Louise looked out of one of the second-floor windows she was cleaning. "Alice, if she keeps singing like that, I'm moving back to Philadelphia. I swear it."

Jane scowled up at her. "Spoilsport."

"Music lover," Louise corrected.

In the guest rooms, they set out blue vases of red and white carnations, and replaced the bud vases in the dining room with teddy bears holding miniature American flags. Jane offered blueberry pancakes for breakfast and garnished them with stars made of raspberry jam or powdered sugar, and brought out pitchers of iced cinnamon tea and pink lemonade for any visitors who stopped by.

Ethel and Lloyd came over to help with the most time-consuming task, hanging the outdoor streamers from the eaves and in the garden. Although everyone started out with a cheerful attitude, when Lloyd mentioned seeing Henry and Patsy in town, spirits quickly plummeted.

"It's not fair," Jane said to Ethel as she tugged down an edge of the red, white and blue streamer from the top of an ivy trellis. "Of all the people for this to happen to, why them?"

"They promised to come back to visit regularly," Alice said as she tied plastic blue and red bows speckled with white stars on the arms of the garden benches. "And they might be able to move back someday."

"The board will have to find a new associate pastor for the church now, too." Ethel didn't seem very enthusiastic.

"I don't imagine it will be as difficult as it was hiring Pastor Thompson," Louise said, "and he has proven to be a very effective minister."

"Maybe this one won't go around breaking family heirlooms," Lloyd tried to joke. "Did you ever find the other one, Alice?"

She went blank at first. "The other . . . oh, you mean the matching cameo vase." She shook her head. "Louise and I have both looked for it, but it's never turned up."

Ethel looked concerned. "You don't think Mr. Alcott's poor mother might have taken that and hidden it somewhere, too?"

"It's possible," Jane said before Alice could reply. "But we don't have time to go looking around for missing vases—we've got an inn to decorate, and a festival to put on, and songs to sing."

"I'll pack my bags," Louise threatened. "I'll be on the first train out tonight. I'll even make you drive me to the station."

Alice laughed at the joke but couldn't help noticing the strained note in her younger sister's voice. This wasn't the first time Jane had changed the subject when someone mentioned the cameo vase, as if she was deliberately trying to avoid talking about it. Then she saw Jane giving her a surreptitious look.

Maybe she's worried talking about it will make me start feeling guilty again. She felt like saying, "Too late."

"Drat this thing." Ethel had lost hold of the streamer and was trying to grab it, but the breeze teased her by fluttering it just out of reach over her head.

"I'll get it," Lloyd said, but he had to stand on his toes, and nearly fell over twice before he caught it.

"Where is Pastor Thompson?" Ethel demanded. "He's the only one around here who's taller than Jane."

Jane winked at her aunt. "He's taller, but I hear he can't sing any better than I can."

"Let's not ever confirm that rumor," Louise said. "As for Pastor Thompson, he checked out last night. He is busy moving into the rectory."

"I offered to help, but he said he wanted to do it himself." Now Jane looked depressed. "I'm going to miss making that pot of decaf in the morning."

"You can make some for me," Louise told her wryly, "but I know what you mean. It was nice having a man around the house again."

"And what am I?" Lloyd pretended to be insulted. "A little old lady?"

Her sisters and aunt laughed and began teasing Lloyd. Alice knew she should have joined in, but she felt a little discouraged. She blamed the shift she had worked the previous evening—she had spent a good part of it going over Mrs. Murphy's chart, trying to recall any possibility of a mistake on her part—but the image of the shattered vase kept popping up in her head. So did her aunt's shocked reproach when she discovered the broken pieces: "If Daniel were here to see this, it would break his heart."

Alice felt that she should have looked for the other vase

before now. Maybe after the Summer Festival she could take down the other books in his study to see if Mrs. Alcott had hidden the vase in another spot. She dreaded going in to work, and even the prospect of the Summer Festival made her feel weary. She wanted to see the kids do well with their play, and she enjoyed spending time with her sisters, but it wouldn't be the same without her father.

Louise went over to help her with the bows. "Tired?"

"Not really." She straightened and put one hand to the small of her back. "I was just thinking about Father, and how this will be the first Summer Festival we've celebrated without him."

"He'll be here in spirit, you know." Louise took the next bow from her and patted her hand. "How are things going with your group's play?"

"Just fine. Pastor Thompson is a big inspiration for the kids." Which was also a bit depressing—Alice felt completely unnecessary now that he was working with the youth. Still, to be fair, he was very good at it, and she added, "He's not like Father was—you know how much the kids loved him—but just the same, he's really good with them. He's always challenging them, getting them to think and to solve their own problems by talking about them."

"He leads through guidance," Louise said, "and that's just another form of love."

"He's doing so much with the program for the Summer Festival, too," Alice admitted. "Since this is one of my days off, I was planning to be at rehearsals today, but he told me I've been working too hard. He said he would supervise the kids this afternoon and that I should stay home and rest for a change." She looked at a bow she had tied onto the bench upside-down and grinned at her own mistake. "*Hmm*, maybe he's right."

"I am impressed." Louise helped her straighten the bow. "Father could never get you to take a day off."

"He never took a day off himself." Alice shaded her eyes and looked out toward the church. Despite Kenneth's insistence that she stay home, she still wanted to watch the kids during the dress rehearsal. "I think I'll take a walk."

"Would you mind postponing that until later?" Louise nodded toward a man and a small group of elementary school kids walking toward the inn. "I think that is Pastor Ley with those children."

It was Henry, Louise saw as she and her sisters came out to greet the group, who quickly assembled into two lines on the porch. "Good afternoon, Pastor Ley, children."

"Good afternoon, Mrs. Smith," the youngsters said in chorus.

"Hello, L-Louise," Henry said. "We have a f-favor to ask. J-Jimmy?"

One of the sixth graders stepped forward. "The bigger kids are using the church right now, Mrs. Smith, and Pastor Ken said we could ask you if we could rehearse our song for the opening of the Summer Festival here."

"Of course you may, children." Louise opened the front door. "Jane, would you take them to the parlor?"

"This way, kids." Her younger sister ushered them inside, with Alice bringing up the rear.

Since she hadn't seen Henry since before the storm, Louise waited behind so she could speak with him privately. "Henry, I just wanted to tell you that we are all so sorry about your leaving Acorn Hill. You have been such a wonderful pastor, and Patsy is so lovely, and none of us can bear to see you go."

"Thank you, L-Louise." He shuffled his feet shyly. "P-Patsy and I have n-never felt m-more b-blessed by our f-friends t-than we d-do now."

She accompanied him to the parlor, where Alice and Jane had the children seated on the floor. As Henry and Louise came in, they jumped to their feet.

"Will you play the music for our song, Mrs. Smith?" one girl asked. "Pastor Ken said you might know the song."

A boy beside her smiled. "Yes, please, Mrs. Smith?"

Jane gave her a wink. "I said you might do it, if they asked nicely and said please."

That produced a unanimous "please" from the children. Louise chuckled. "I would be delighted to accompany you, children." She turned to Henry. "What song are the children performing?"

"'A-America' by S-Samuel Francis S-Smith," Henry said.

"Miss Howard and I will be your audience," Jane said, and sat down in front of the choir. "And if you sing really, really well, I think there might be a little snack for everyone afterward."

The children cheered and chattered and bounced with excitement, but settled down when they saw Louise take her place at the piano. When they were ready, she nodded to Henry and played the opening bars to the old and beloved song.

With his mellow tenor, he sang the first line, "My country, 'tis of thee . . ."

The youngsters followed, adding the sweet young voices to his:

Sweet land of liberty,
Of thee I sing.
Land where my fathers died,
Land of the pilgrims' pride,
From every mountain side
Let freedom ring.

Louise was pleased with how well the children's voices followed her piano and Henry's strong tenor. The youthful choir had been Patsy's idea, and she and Henry had been working with the children for the last several weeks.

My native country, thee,
Land of the noble free,
Thy name I love;
I love thy rocks and rills,
Thy woods and templed hills;
My heart with rapture thrills
Like that above.

Ethel and Lloyd slipped in to join Alice and Jane as part of the audience.

Let music swell the breeze,
And ring from all the trees
Sweet freedom's song;
Let mortal tongues awake,
Let all that breathe partake,
Let rocks their silence break—
The sound prolong.

The last verse was Louise's favorite of the whole song, for it was not only part of the lyrics, but also a lovely prayer in itself.

"Our fathers' God, to Thee,
Author of liberty,
To Thee we sing,
Long may our land be bright
With freedom's holy light;
Protect us by Thy might,
Great God, our King."

As the last notes Louise played drifted into silence, Ethel, Lloyd and both of her sisters got to their feet and applauded enthusiastically.

Louise rose from the piano bench to do the same, and

smiled at Henry. "I don't know who told you that you had to practice," she said to the children. "That was, without a doubt, the loveliest rendition of 'America' that I have ever heard."

"You know what that means, kids." Jane waggled her brows at the children. "Cookies and juice for everyone!"

With another round of cheers the youngsters followed Jane out of the parlor. Alice and Ethel went along to help with the refreshments.

"Henry." Lloyd shook the minister's hand. "We're sure going to miss you around here."

Louise turned to the mayor. "Isn't there something we can do, Lloyd? Perhaps start a house-building fund . . . ?"

"D-don't worry, L-Louise," Henry told her. He gave her a distinctly mysterious smile. "I have f-faith that w-with God's h-help, e-everything will w-w-ork out in th-the end."

Alice enjoyed watching Henry's chorus demolish Jane's entire chocolate chip cookie supply, and drink up every drop of apple and orange juice in the refrigerator. It was impossible to feel blue with so many happy little faces around her. After Henry reminded them to thank the sisters politely for the snack, Ethel gave them permission to play a game of freeze-tag on the lawn.

"Have you ever noticed how most kids only have two speeds when they're awake?" Jane asked as they watched the children play their energetic game with much shrieking and laughing.

Alice chuckled. "No, I haven't. What are they?"

"Stop and go."

She thought of Bobby Dawson, who was never still. "You might want to come to my next meeting with the kids at church, little sister."

"They make me feel hot and tired, just watching them." Ethel fanned herself with her hat, and smiled as Louise,

Lloyd and Henry joined them. "But they do sing like angels, Henry."

The associate pastor thanked Ethel and the sisters again, and then called the children together to walk back to the church with him. Ethel and Lloyd decided to go into town to do some shopping before the weekend, and also departed.

Alice forced herself to help her sisters clear up after the children, and then surreptitiously checked the time.

The rehearsal should be in full swing by now. "If you don't need me for anything else, I think I'll take that walk now," she said, and patted her hip. "I have to work off Jane's cookies."

"I'll have to report you to Pastor Ken," Jane said, "for not putting up your feet and relaxing, like he told you to."

"Oh, you know me." She gave a little laugh. "Never happy unless I'm doing something."

Louise gave her a sharp look and handed her a straw hat. "Put this on and don't go too far, Alice. You do look a little peaked, and you'll end up with heat exhaustion."

"I'll be careful." She put on the hat and set off across the lawn.

Daniel Howard had actually created the path from his home to Grace Chapel by walking there to pray every day. As Alice followed the trail he had worn smooth over the years, she missed him more acutely than she ever had since his death.

It's always the simple things that make me wish you were here, Father. Drinking lemonade on the porch or watching the kids play on the lawn. She looked down at her own sensible shoes. *Or trying to walk in your footsteps.*

As she drew near the back of the church, she heard the voices of the children through the windows Kenneth had left open in the Assembly Room. Rather than interrupt them, she decided to slip in quietly and see how things were going without distracting the youngsters from their performance.

All the children were in costume and standing in their

positions as they would be in the front of the church, where the stage would be set up on the night of the program. In the center stood two boys dressed in plain tunics. They held a large net between them filled with plastic fish. Off to the right were girls dressed in simple robes and carrying empty baskets.

"So one day, I'm minding my own business and bringing in my catch from the Sea of Galilee," one of the fishermen recited, "and who do you think comes up to me?"

The girls with the baskets spoke in unison. "Who, Peter?"

"Some fella named Jesus." The boy playing Peter laughed. "He walked right up to me and my brother Andrew—hey, Andy, remember what he said?"

"He said we should come and follow him," the boy playing Andrew let out a theatrical sigh. "I thought he said he would make us better *fishermen*."

"But that's not what he said," the girls said, shaking their heads and smiling.

"Nope," said Peter. "Jesus said he would make us fishers of men. And then you know what me and my crazy brother did? We laid down out fishing nets—left them right there on the shore—and followed Jesus."

"Stop there." Alice heard Pastor Thompson say. "That's very good, you didn't miss a single line. Now, when Charles comes out from stage right, remember to follow him around the stage, just as Peter and Andrew followed Jesus."

"Can we put down our baskets, too, Pastor Ken?" one of the girls asked.

Alice could see the new minister had everything completely under control. She was proud of how closely the children were listening to him and how well the rehearsal was going, but she also felt more useless than ever. Silently she retreated before she was noticed and left the church.

She hardly realized where her feet were taking her until

minutes later she stood in the little cemetery where they had buried Daniel the previous year. It was an easy walk from the church to the quiet little place. She and her sisters had been visiting his grave regularly to keep it neat and to leave fresh flowers from the garden. Today, however, she had come empty-handed, so all she could do was bend over to brush some grass clippings away from the base of his headstone.

"Hi, Father." She knelt down on the grass, but a peeping sound from overhead made her look up. A pair of wrens had taken up residence in the oak tree that shaded this corner of the cemetery, and their merry chirping usually cheered her. Now it only seemed to underscore how flat and unhappy her thoughts had been. "I wish you were here. I could sure use a hug and a good talking-to."

From the cemetery Alice could see both Grace Chapel Inn and the church for which they had named it. Daniel Howard had been laid to rest within sight of them, alongside the wife he had loved so dearly; and when she looked over at her mother's grave, tears flowed into Alice's eyes, and she finally let go of the words she had been holding inside for so long.

"I've been trying to cope with everything, Father, but there are times when I don't think I can." She traced the letters of her father's name on the headstone. "Just as I think I'm finally getting over the shock of losing you, something happens, and the memories knock me down." She glanced in the direction of the inn. "I should have known how special that cameo vase was, and how much it meant to you and Mother. But I didn't, and now I haven't even looked hard enough to find the other one. I'm really sorry about that."

She took a deep breath and looked in the direction of the church. The children were leaving in pairs and small groups, some going to their parents waiting in cars outside, some walking together toward town.

"I thought I was doing well with the youth ministry, but

with work and running the inn, I haven't devoted the proper amount of time to the children. I think they're drifting away from me, Father."

A tree branch trembled as the wrens suddenly flew out of the oak tree.

"I've always wanted to be a positive force in their lives, but Pastor Thompson seems so much better at it." Tears finally spilled down her face. "And that poor woman at the hospital—that's the worst thing of all. What if I've been so busy rushing around that I did make a mistake? She'll be all right, but drug reactions can kill people. If I'm responsible for what happened to her. . . ." She didn't want to think about what she would do then. "I've been trying to do my best, but I feel like I'm really messing up and disappointing everyone."

She took her handkerchief out of her pocket and wiped her eyes. A strange sense of peace settled over her, and for a moment she thought it was because she had finally had the courage to admit her feelings of guilt and failure out loud. Then she saw that one of the wrens had glided down to perch on the top of her father's headstone. It cocked its head and studied her with its bright black eyes, as if wondering why she was crying.

When Alice was a girl, Daniel often brought her and her sisters here to put flowers on her mother's grave. He was never sad, however, even when he prayed with his daughters for God to watch over their beloved Madeleine.

As she looked back at the little bird, one of Daniel's verses came back to her, "Cast thy burden upon the Lord, and he shall sustain thee: he shall never suffer the righteous to be moved."

She could almost hear her father's voice telling her the same thing, "It's time to turn this over to God, Alice."

Maybe it is. She folded her hands and bowed her head to pray. "Dear Lord, You have showed so much mercy to the world. Please bless the souls of my father and mother, and let them be together forever in paradise. Help me to be the woman they raised me to be, and guide me always with Your truth and light. Through Jesus Christ, our Lord, I pray. Amen."

When Alice opened her eyes, she felt much better—as if a terrible weight had been lifted from her shoulders. The little wren chirped at her, then spread its wings and flew back up to the oak tree.

"I agree." She got up slowly and dusted off her trousers before turning toward Grace Chapel Inn. "It's time to go home."

∞

Alice slept better that night than she had in weeks, and woke the next morning to the sound of gentle tapping on her bedroom door. Yawning, she sat up and saw that it was more than an hour before the time she usually rose. "Come in."

Louise opened the door and peeked cautiously inside. "I'm sorry to disturb you, but there's a doctor downstairs, and he says that he needs to speak to you, right away."

Bewildered, Alice put on her robe and slippers before following her sister downstairs, where a tired-looking man wearing gold-rimmed glasses was waiting by the front desk.

"Ms. Howard." It was Mrs. Murphy's physician. "I probably should have called, but I'm on my way to the airport for a business trip, and I wanted to see you before I left."

"It's no trouble at all, Doctor." Alice fought back the feeling of dread. "Is it about Mrs. Murphy?"

"Yes, I was called in last night on her case, after she had gone into anaphylactic shock. We nearly lost her twice before we were able to stabilize her condition."

Alice knew that kind of trauma was caused by severe allergic reaction, generally to drugs. She swallowed. "Doctor, I went over everything I did, and I had another nurse check my notes. I can't imagine what I did, but—"

"That's the reason I'm here, Ms. Howard. You didn't do anything." He looked a little sheepish. "After we were able to stabilize her, her husband admitted that he had brought her some food from her favorite restaurant. You know Mrs. Murphy was on a strict diet because of the medications she was taking. Unfortunately, what he brought her reacted with one of the drugs I prescribed, producing the rash first, and the trauma last night."

Alice felt like sagging with relief. "Will Mrs. Murphy be all right?"

The doctor nodded. "I expect her to make a full recovery, now that I know where the problem lies. I just wanted to come here and apologize to you for my insinuations. The other nurses on the ward assured me that you could not have been responsible, but I didn't believe them, and as a result I wasn't very fair to you." He sighed. "I am sorry I blamed you, Ms. Howard. I know what that must have put you through."

"Please, don't apologize. If the situation were reversed, I would have been just as concerned for the patient." She smiled. "And thank you for taking the time to come and tell me in person."

The doctor shook her hand. "And if I can presume to ask, if you would keep an eye on Mrs. Murphy for me while I'm out of town, I would appreciate it."

"I will, Doctor."

After Alice saw him out, she and Louise stood by the front window, watching the airport taxi drive away.

"You never said anything about this." Louise put an arm around her shoulders. "You should have, you know. That is what family is for."

"I know, I should have. But I talked to Father about it yesterday," she said, and smiled a little. "So in a way, I did."

Chapter Fourteen

As the first morning of Summer Festival weekend arrived, Louise and Alice came downstairs to find a buffet already set up and waiting in the dining room for their guests.

"My goodness, Jane must have gotten up at dawn to do this," Alice said. "Why didn't she tell us about her plans?"

"You know how Jane is when she gets an early start. Damn the torpedoes, full speed ahead." Louise smiled. "We will have to make breakfast for her for a change."

Yet when they went into the kitchen, there was no sign of Jane. All the dishes were washed and put away, and the counters were sparkling clean.

"Look at this." Louise picked up a note in Jane's neat handwriting, which she had left on the kitchen table beside a full teapot kept warm in a cozy.

"She hasn't run away from home, I hope."

"It says: 'Ignore the morning paper.'" Louise read out loud. "'Pour yourselves some tea and bring it out to the garden. We're going to have a picnic.'" She set down the note. "We're having a picnic? At 7:00 A.M.?"

Alice looked through the window and saw Jane sitting with a huge basket on an oversized red and white picnic cloth on the lawn. "Apparently Jane is."

"Good Lord, what is she doing, going through her second childhood?" Louise handed her younger sister a mug as she peered out.

"A picnic ..." Alice concentrated for a moment, then her expression lit up. "I know. She's having a breakfast picnic. Remember how Mother used to do that for us?"

"Yes, but we were just little girls." Louise glanced back at the kitchen table. "I am far too old to be sitting on the ground before I've had my first cup of coffee."

"No, you're not. Get moving." Alice gave her a gentle push toward the garden door.

When she heard the door close, Jane looked up and smiled at them. "Morning, Louise, Alice." She began unpacking the picnic hamper and setting places on the picnic cloth for them. "Welcome to the first day of the Summer Festival. Bring your appetites over here and sit down."

"What brought on this idea?" Louise asked as she carefully sat down next to her sister.

"I was reading through some of Father's old papers. You know, from the box Fred brought from the rectory? Among them I found a letter to his parents that he had never finished, describing the breakfast picnic Mother always made for you and Alice every Fourth of July." She handed Louise a corn muffin. "Since I was never invited to one, I decided to revive the tradition and hold my own."

"It must have taken a lot of work to do this and make the buffet for the guests." Alice added some honey and butter to her muffin. "We would have been happy to help."

Their younger sister smiled. "Oh, I had help. Here comes my co-conspirator now."

"Happy Independence Day, girls!" Ethel walked up the path from the carriage house. She wore a smart-looking navy dress topped off with a straw hat with festive red, white and blue stars around the base of the crown. "Well, were they surprised, Jane?"

"I think so." To her sisters, she said, "Aunt Ethel gave me all the details on what our mother used to do. She had all the insider info."

"Did you also tell Jane how Mother had potato sack races, water balloon fights and egg tosses with us after lunch?" Alice asked with a twinkle in her eye.

"There will be no potato sack races, no filling of balloons with water—and the first person who so much as looks at an egg is spending the day locked in her room." Louise glared at her sister in mock anger.

"Oh, lighten up, Louie." A sly smile crossed Jane's face as she resurrected that pet name she used to use to tease her older sister.

"I don't remember *Mother* threatening us at the annual breakfast picnic." Alice laughed softly and then looked up as two of their guests came out of the side door. "Um, we may have to postpone our little family celebration to take care of our guests."

"No, we won't." Jane grinned as she laid out two more place settings. "Because I invited the guests to join us, too."

The fine weather and Jane's impromptu picnic put the sisters and their aunt in such a good mood that they decided to walk into town for the opening Summer Festival ceremony and town parade. Along the way, the sisters stopped by the mayor's house to collect Lloyd, who had put on one of his favorite white suits and added a gaily striped red, white and blue tie.

"Good morning, girls. You're all looking lovely today." He presented Ethel with a gorgeous old-fashioned corsage made of three delicate red rosebuds and white and blue satin ribbons. "And these are for you, beautiful lady."

"What's this for?" she asked, surprised.

He smiled at her. "I want everyone to see who my girl is."

She blushed. "I'm too old to be your girl." But as he pinned the corsage to her lapel, her eyes sparkled with pleasure. The streets and sidewalks of Acorn Hill were crowded with tourists and townspeople alike. All of the local shopkeepers had put up patriotic displays in honor of the holiday, and the Coffee Shop had set up a refreshments stand and a large booth for the traditional pie-eating contest.

"Charles Matthews has sworn to win first place this year," Alice said, nodding toward the golden brown pies that Hope Collins was stacking on the booth's long table. "I think he wants revenge for coming in second to his sister last year."

"I've seen Sissy Matthews eat," Jane said, shaking her head. "That skinny little girl can put away more food than three grown men put together. He doesn't stand a chance."

"Ms. Howard!" Bobby Dawson ran up to them and skidded to a stop. "Have you seen Pastor Ken?"

"Not yet, Bobby. Is there something I can do?"

"Well, it's about the—" Bobby did something odd then: his mouth snapped shut and his eyes widened. He recovered a moment later and forced a grin. "No, thank you, ma'am. It's just something I needed to ask him." He dashed away, dodging people on the sidewalks.

Alice laughed. "You were wrong, Jane. Some kids only have one speed—go."

The opening ceremony was about to begin, so Lloyd excused himself to go to the special podium set up in front of Fred's Hardware store. The sisters and their aunt found places in the rows of folding chairs Fred had provided, and stood as the town's American flag was raised. Lloyd led everyone in the Pledge of Allegiance, and then gave a short speech about the history of Acorn Hill and how the town represented so many of the wonderful freedoms that they enjoyed as Americans.

"We are truly blessed to be citizens of this town and our great nation," he said at the end. "As Mayor of Acorn Hill,

I thank you all for coming out to share this celebration of freedom with us today. God Bless America!"

As everyone applauded, Henry Ley's choir filed out onto the podium platform, and Lloyd adjusted the microphone for them. The townspeople applauded wildly as soon as Henry stepped up to lead the children in their song, and for a moment, tears stung Louise's eyes

Dear Lord, please look after him and Patsy, wherever they go from here.

After the choir finished their song to more thundering applause, the chairs were cleared away and everyone lined both sides of the street to watch the annual town parade. A band from the area high school came marching along stepping smartly. They were followed by clowns, dancers, and members of the local veterans' association in their various dress uniforms. A car decorated with flowers and bearing the winners of a local beauty pageant drove slowly behind the veterans, followed by majorettes twirling batons. A performer on stilts dressed as Uncle Sam tossed wrapped candy to the watching children.

"Jane!" Alice laughed in protest as her younger sister jumped up to snatch a foil-wrapped chocolate for herself. "Those are for the kids."

"Hey, this is free candy." She waggled her prize under her sister's nose. "It's every kid for herself."

Spectators shouted and waved miniature American flags as they cheered the participants, from the first band to the last performer. When the parade was over, Lloyd made a few last announcements from the podium.

"And don't forget to come and see this evening's program, *Gone Fishing*, seven o'clock at Grace Chapel," he added. "Tickets are still on sale at the refreshment stand, and all proceeds will go toward the youth ministry mission."

The sisters went around to see friends in town and inspect the various stands and displays. Louise was surprised to learn that Fred Humbert had been working in secret for nearly a year to build a scale model of the entire town, which included a tiny creek with real running water.

"This is amazing," she told Vera as she inspected the perfectly detailed shops and houses. Even the church and Grace Chapel Inn had been reproduced exactly. "I had no idea Fred possessed a gift for this kind of detailed work."

"He's made models since he was a boy," Vera said, "but he only used them for Christmas displays. Actually, it was your father who gave him the idea for this project. After the festival, Fred plans to donate it to the town hall as a permanent display. He wants to add a few more lights and some sound effects boxes to it."

Jane crouched down to look inside the little replica of the inn. "Hey, I can see a teeny little brunette in there, slaving over a tiny little hot stove." She cocked her head. "And I think she's singing."

"You might want to have Fred apply a little duct tape here and there, too," Louise advised Vera.

Tables were set up in a lot behind the Coffee Shop for the town barbecue, which ran all afternoon. Louise and her sisters stayed to watch the pie-eating contest, which, as predicted, Sissy Matthews won for the second year in a row.

Ribbons were handed out by the judges for the different contests, and Jane won first place in the bakery category with her entry of the friendship bread, the recipe for which she had finally conquered.

"I can't believe it. I won!" She showed her sisters the blue ribbon. "I've never won a ribbon for anything before."

Louise was amused by her enthusiastic reaction. "You were a chef in a five-star restaurant, Jane. It's not exactly fair."

"My being a chef isn't cheating. Besides, that recipe was

tough. I thought I was going to kick the oven a few times while I was working it out."

Louise sighed. "You did, dear. At least twice."

"Aunt Ethel's peach tarts won first place in the dessert category," Alice reported. "Again."

Jane got a gleam in her eye. "*This* year."

Alice patted her sister on the shoulder. "If anyone can find a way to oust Aunt Ethel's tarts, it'll be you, Jane."

Louise caught a glimpse of Pastor Thompson coming out of Acorn Hill Antiques, and looked puzzled. "Did the Holzmanns come back from Europe early?"

"No, as far as I know they're still there." Alice followed her gaze and watched as Pastor Thompson took out a set of keys and locked the door to the antique shop. "Now that's odd. What was he doing in there, and why does he have keys?"

"I don't know." Louise spotted a brown-wrapped package under his arm. "Maybe he's watching the shop for the Holzmanns."

Jane took her sisters' arms. "I'm thirsty and I want to celebrate my victory. Let's go over to the Coffee Shop and wet our whistles, my treat."

After enjoying three tall lemonades, the sisters headed back to the inn. Once she had made sure their guests would be set for the evening, Alice decided to change and go over to Grace Chapel early. It turned out to be a wise decision, for when she arrived she found the sanctuary in a state of barely controlled chaos.

Only about half of the cast had arrived, and they were in various states of dress. Some were in costume; others had brought theirs with them and were still wearing their regular clothes.

"Pastor Ken! Pastor Ken!" Bobby was running back and forth across the stage that had been set up at the front of the chapel, and as he ran he darted around the other children and waved his fishing pole like a sword. "Watch me cast!"

"In a moment, Bobby." Kenneth was trying to move a large backdrop behind the altar with the help of three of the older children, but the children were bickering and trying to pull it in different directions. For the first time since Alice had met the minister, he looked on the edge of losing his temper, and yet he kept his voice patient as he said, "Children, move your side to the right. No, your other right."

In sharp contrast, Charles Matthews was sitting on the edge of the stage, holding his hands to the sides of his head. He was also groaning, as if in pain.

Alice went up to him first. "Charles? What's wrong?"

"I don't feel so good, Ms. Howard." He lifted his pale face and grimaced as he pressed a hand to his abdomen. "My stomach is really upset."

Bobby rushed over to the edge of the stage. "Watch me, Ms. Howard, I can play the part of the fisherman."

"Mom told you not to try to beat me," Charles's unsympathetic sister said to him. "Eating too much pie always makes you sick."

Charles scowled. "Oh, shut up, Sissy!" Then he paled and covered his mouth to muffle a low belch. "Ms. Howard, can you die from eating too much blueberry pie?"

"No, Charles." Alice suppressed a smile. "You will feel you want to for a few hours, but it wears off."

"I told you so," Sissy said, sounding exactly like Jane.

"Sissy, please." Alice helped the boy to his feet. "We'd better get you home and into bed."

Kenneth was still trying to maneuver the backdrop, when he noticed Alice and gave her a hurried greeting. She returned his greeting but turned away quickly as she noticed that more children were obviously getting restless. Alice didn't even think twice about it when she stepped up on the stage to get things under control.

"Robert Dawson," she said in her severest tone. "Go and sit down in the first pew." As Bobby reluctantly left the stage, she helped Charles to the door. "You can go and sit quietly in the vesting room until your mother gets here."

"But what about the play, Ms. Howard? I'm supposed to be the fisherman," Charles protested in a weak voice.

"I'll take care of that." She gestured to his sister. "Sissy, go with Charles to the vesting room and call your mother. Tell her that your brother is not feeling well, and ask her to come right away." She eyed the boy's face. "And put the waste basket by his side, in case your brother needs to use it."

"Yes, ma'am." Sissy took her brother's arm. "Next year you have to enter the watermelon eating contest. Watermelon never makes you sick."

"Does, too," Charles protested as his sister led him away.

The other children started crowding around Alice, protesting that without Charles the play would be ruined. She clapped her hands twice, very loudly, and their voices fell silent.

"Charles is not feeling well, and we can't expect him to try to perform when he's sick. Anyone who is not in costume, please go and change in the restroom immediately." She scanned the stage. "Does someone have a copy of the script?" She smiled as one of the younger girls handed her a copy. "Very good. Now, I want to see all the villagers here, stage left."

Once the other children had returned from changing, she organized everyone on the stage. "While Pastor Thompson is getting the props in place, we're going to do a quick run-through of your lines. Take your places now. We'll start from the beginning. Don't worry about moving around the stage, just stay where you are and recite your lines."

"What about me, Ms. Howard?" Bobby called tearfully from the front pew. "Can't I be the fisherman?"

"I have a very special job for you." Alice gestured for him to come up on stage, and handed him the script. "I want you to listen to everyone's lines, and check to make sure they're correct. Would you do that for me?"

Bobby beamed. "I sure will!"

Once the kids had started reciting, Alice went over to help Kenneth with the backdrop, which they still had not gotten into place. The problem was that the backdrop was so large that the pastor literally could not see where they were going with it. "Jessica, Gena, Stephen, stop elbowing each other and get serious. We have to move this into place before the audience begins to arrive." She turned to Kenneth. "I'll take your side, Pastor, if you'll step back and direct us where to place it."

Kenneth nodded with visible relief. "Thank you, Alice." He stepped back. "All right, we need to move it back a few inches away from the curtains, then slide it to the right. That's it. Another inch back on the left, there, Stephen."

With the backdrop in place, Kenneth began arranging props and Alice took over supervising the children who had finished changing, and sending others to change as they arrived. In between she kept an eye on Bobby and listened to the players reciting their lines. Someone had changed some of the scenes, she realized, but she was too busy checking costumes to concentrate on the exact words.

When the audience began to arrive, Alice led everyone backstage and lifted a finger to her lips. "Now, until it's time to go on, we should all be very quiet."

"What about Charles's part?" one of the girls asked.

"I can be the fisherman!" Bobby declared. The other kids shushed him, and he made a face as he lowered his voice to a comical stage whisper. "I can."

"You're too short." Sissy whispered back fiercely. "You won't be able to cast for the fish."

"We'll figure something out," Alice promised them. "Now, before we put on the program, let's have a moment of prayer to thank the Lord for this wonderful day."

Kenneth came back shortly after that. "We're ready up front."

"We're all ready here, too." She smiled at the grinning faces around her. "But Charles Matthews won't be able to perform his role, and we need a new fisherman." She leaned forward and lowered her voice. "Bobby would like to, but he is too short, and if he casts out into the audience, people are going to get hurt."

Kenneth frowned and nodded. "That's going to be tough. I didn't assign anyone as an understudy, and I don't think any of the other boys are familiar enough with Charles's lines to carry it off."

She smiled. "That's why you'll have to take over the part, Pastor."

"Me?" He looked startled.

"There's no one who knows the part better than the minister who wrote it." She eyed his immaculate jacket and snowy white dress shirt and tie. "We do have a bit of a problem, though—Charles's costume won't fit you."

"That's true." The new minister thought for a moment, then smiled. "But I know someone who might provide me with just what I need."

Chapter 🪟 Fifteen

Louise and Jane took their places in the audience beside Ethel and Lloyd. The entire church was packed, and Fred was still setting up folding chairs at the back.

It was wonderful to see Grace Chapel filled again, Louise thought. Not since Daniel's death had so many people come to the little church.

"Have you seen Alice?" Ethel asked Louise.

"No, but she's probably going to stay backstage with the children." Louise turned as Henry Ley came out and everyone fell quiet.

"Good e-evening, ladies and g-gentlemen." For once the associate pastor seemed not to be self-conscious, and he even smiled at the audience. "W-welcome to our Summer F-Festival. The children have a w-wonderful show for y-you tonight, so sit b-back and e-enjoy."

Everyone applauded as Henry left the stage and the lights dimmed. A spotlight clicked on, and two boys dressed in period costumes came out, hauling an empty fishing net between them.

"No fish today," one of the boys said, making a comically glum face. "Why do we keep on fishing if we never catch anything?"

"I don't know," his companion said, and sighed dramatically. "Maybe we should give up."

"Give up?" A deep voice said from the shadows. "Why, you haven't even done any real fishing yet."

The audience burst out with laughter as Pastor Thompson strode onto the stage. He was wearing one of his pressed dressed shirts with the sleeves rolled up, and had done the same to his immaculate navy blue suit trousers. On his head was an old rumpled hat with fishing lures tied to it, and over his shirt he wore a faded khaki vest with lots of pockets.

Louise's eyes widened as she recognized the hat and the vest. "Is that . . . ?"

"Yes," Jane grinned, "I suspect our aunt is involved in this." The hat and vest had belonged to their father, who had looked just as comical in them.

The new minister took off his hat and shook it at their empty net. "You're complaining because you didn't catch any fish on one day?"

"We didn't catch any yesterday, either," one boy said, as he looked very indignant.

"Or the day before that," the other added. "And we tried really hard."

Kenneth threw his arms out. "Do you boys even know what it takes to be a good fisherman?"

The boys looked at each other before one of them replied, "A bigger net?"

"A bigger net." The new minister shook his head sadly. "No wonder you haven't caught anything."

A young girl hurried out from the wings and whispered something to the other boy, who said, "Faith? What's that got to do with fishing?"

The rest of the cast filed out onto the stage. As the children acted out humorous adaptations of several stories from the Bible, the minister continued appearing as the Master Fisherman, challenging the boys to state what they had learned from their experiences. The combination had the audience constantly in stitches.

Pastor Thompson also demonstrated his skill with a rod and reel when he began to distribute Bible-verse fish to the audience. With swift, deceptively easy movements of his arm, he cast out the fishing line. It extended in a wide arc over the heads of the audience until Kenneth snapped his wrist, causing a plastic fish to drop neatly into someone's hands.

Not realizing that the line was descending toward her, Ethel leaned forward to retrieve a hanky from her purse. Kenneth jerked the line and narrowly avoided having the fish land on her head, then expertly deposited the fish in her purse as she straightened. She made a startled sound, then shook the fish at the pastor and joined in the laughter around her.

Toward the end of the play, Lloyd excused himself and slipped out of the sanctuary.

Louise leaned over to ask Ethel if the mayor was all right, but at that moment her aunt pointed toward Alice, standing just offstage with Kenneth.

"There she is," she whispered. "I was hoping he could get her to where she could see."

"To see what?" Louise murmured, but her aunt only lifted a finger to her lips, and then pointed to the stage.

Two young actors announced that they were going fishing, and left the stage. The lights came up, and applause started as it seemed the play had ended.

Louise frowned. "Isn't Pastor Kenneth going to close the program with prayer?"

Ethel chuckled. "Not exactly."

The applause stopped suddenly when three little girls walked out hand in hand. Louise was startled to see they resembled Jane, Alice and herself when each of them had been about six or seven years old. The similarity was remarkable, right down to the clothes they were wearing.

"Hey," Jane murmured, staring at the smallest girl, who was wearing a flowery hat. "She looks like I did when I was in the first grade."

Ethel leaned over. "I thought I remembered the clothes right."

A familiar-looking figure walked out onto the stage. It was Lloyd, but he was dressed in one of her father's old cardigans. "Well, girls, we can't go fishing today—the weather is too bad," he said, doing a wonderful imitation of Daniel Howard. "What would you like to do instead?"

"I'd like to play veterinarian," the girl dressed as Alice said. "Can I give our tabby a check-up?"

"I have to practice for my recital," the one pretending to be Louise said, flexing her fingers.

The girl playing Jane stamped her foot. "I want to go on an adventure!" That made everyone chuckle. "Can we go and hunt tigers in the forest? I know, let's get our fishing poles and sneak out to the creek, Father."

"Oh, Lord," Jane mumbled, coloring. "Did I really stamp my feet like that?"

"Constantly," Louise said dryly. "I can show you the old heel marks on the floor."

"I know," little Alice said, and gathered her sisters around her to whisper to them. Little Louise and Jane nodded and the three sisters went to Lloyd, leading him to a chair before they turned to the audience. The girl playing Louise stepped out and recited solemnly:

O Lord, our Lord,
how majestic is Your name in all the earth!
You have set Your glory
above the heavens.
From the lips of children and infants

You have ordained praise
because of Your enemies,
to silence the foe and the avenger.

Little Jane took a toy telescope from her pocket and
peered through it at the ceiling as she recited the next lines
of the beloved old psalm by herself.

When I consider Your heavens,
the work of Your fingers,
the moon and the stars,
which You have set in place,
what is man that You are mindful of him,
the son of man that You care for him?

Finally, the girl playing Alice produced a stuffed toy
tabby cat, which looked remarkably like the pet the real Alice
had had as a child, and cradled it in her arms.

You made him a little lower than the heavenly beings
and crowned him with glory and honor.
You made him ruler over the works of Your hands;
You put everything under his feet:

Together, all three girls finished the last lines. As they
recited the words, they also added the respective animal calls
and movements to act out the animal parts:

all flocks and herds,
and the beasts of the field,
the birds of the air,
and the fish of the sea,
all that swim the paths of the seas.
O Lord, our Lord,
how majestic is Your name in all the earth!

Louise knew every word, of course—it had been Daniel
Howard's favorite psalm—and somehow Ethel had remembered how the three of them would recite it and act out the
animal parts for their father when they were younger. She
looked at Jane, who had her handkerchief out and was blot-
ting her cheeks with it, then at Alice, who was smiling
through joyous tears at the children.

Lloyd came to the center of the stage and knelt down to
receive a hug from all three little girls. He looked out at
Louise and Jane, then over at Alice, and nodded. It was as if
in that moment, Daniel's presence filled the sanctuary.

That brought the audience to their feet, and this time the
applause was so loud that it rattled every window in the
church.

After bringing the entire cast out for several curtain calls,
Pastor Thompson came out into the audience to receive
warm congratulations from the congregation. Alice joined
her sisters in thanking him and their aunt with heartfelt grat-
itude for the special tribute to their father.

"It was the least I could do," Kenneth said modestly.
"Not only for the finest fisher of men who ever lived in Acorn
Hill, but for the daughters who continue his work and have
helped so many." There were people waiting to speak to him,
so he excused himself, adding only, "Would you ladies join
me over at the rectory after we're through here? I'm having a
little house-warming party tonight."

"We'd be delighted to," Jane said, before Alice or Louise
could reply, and Kenneth nodded and turned to shake hands
with Fred Humbert.

"Oh dear." Louise looked at her sister. "We don't have a
house-warming gift to bring."

"We donated all that old furniture, Louie," Jane reminded
her before grinning at Alice. "So, were you surprised?"

"Was I! He never told me a word about the finale he had planned." Alice sighed. "You know something, Pastor Thompson is more like Father than I ever imagined. I just never saw it before."

Since Ethel and Lloyd were also heading for the pastor's party, they all went together from church with joyful chatter. When they arrived at the rectory, Louise spotted Henry and Patsy's car parked in the back and saw the Holzmanns being welcomed at the front door.

"I see Joseph and Rachel are back from Europe. Thank goodness we didn't have a chance to accuse them of buying stolen merchandise a few weeks ago," she whispered to Jane.

Fred and Vera welcomed them in, and Vera informed them where they might find light refreshments.

"Pastor Thompson called to say he'll be here shortly," Fred told the sisters. "And I'm to give you the grand tour."

The old, cluttered rectory had been completely transformed. Fred's handiwork had repaired all the damage to the walls, while the furnishings the Howard sisters and others had donated gave a warm and inviting air to each room.

"Fred, you're a magician," Jane said as she inspected the embossed wallpaper and new white tile installed in the bathroom. "I can hardly believe this is the same place I saw a couple of weeks ago. I want to live here."

He grinned. "Give me a trowel, some cement and a couple of strong backs, Jane, and I'll build you the Taj Mahal out of a molehill."

They all hailed Kenneth when he arrived a few minutes later. He was carrying a gift-wrapped box, which he placed carefully on a side table before greeting them.

"I think tonight went very well, and I thank you all for coming," he said. "Before we begin the last round of festivities, I would like to offer our Lord one more prayer of thanks."

As they all bowed their heads, Kenneth thanked God for their many blessings, and in particular for Alice's tireless work with the ANGELs and other youngsters who took part in the Summer Festival program. After he finished, he took the wrapped box and carried it to Alice.

"I don't understand," Alice said, looking at it with a bewildered expression. "This is your party, Pastor."

He smiled down at her. "But this gift is for you, Alice."

She opened it carefully; then, as she parted the tissue paper, she gasped.

"It's not a puppy, is it?" Jane leaned forward, smiling.

"No, it's not." Carefully, Alice lifted out one delicate column of green and white glass, and then another exactly like it.

Louise saw Jane and the Holzmanns beam at each other, and finally knew what Rachel had been carrying wrapped in one of their kitchen towels that day.

"The cameo vases." She held them carefully, examining the lovely old glass before looking up at Kenneth. "But I broke one of these. Louise and I swept up the pieces and threw them away. How did you . . . ?" she made a helpless gesture.

"Your Aunt Ethel told me how precious these were to your father and your family," the pastor said. "I knew the vases were popular during the Depression, and that it was possible to find a replacement, so I enlisted the help of your sister."

When Alice glanced at her, Louise shook her head. "Not this sister. The other one. The sneaky one."

"I found the other vase in Father's study and gave it to Kenneth," Jane confessed. "He took it to Joseph to see if a matching vase could be located."

"Which wasn't easy," Mr. Holzmann put in. "My wife and I had to keep it for several weeks while we were finding a match." He chuckled. "You gave us quite a start the day you came to deliver that invitation, Louise. Rachel had it in her hands when you came in."

Alice shook her head slowly, smiling. "Jane, I can't believe you never said a word."

"Let me tell you, it wasn't easy," her younger sister assured her, "what with you and Louise searching the house and asking me about it practically every other day. And you know what a terrible liar I am to begin with."

"I'm very grateful, Pastor, and I know my sisters and aunt are, too," Alice said as she carefully placed the precious objects back in the box. "But I'm still a little confused as to why you went to so much trouble—and expense—to replace an old vase."

Kenneth took her hands in his. "Broken vases can often be replaced, Alice, but fathers can't. I want you to know that I will never be able to replace your father, or the many happy memories that he gave you, your sisters and his congregation throughout his life. I know my purpose in coming to Acorn Hill was to follow the same calling as your father did, and to lead others to God. I'm privileged to be able to continue Daniel's lifetime of work by carrying on his ministry." He squeezed her hands. "I hope we can all make many new and happy memories to add to the treasured ones that you already have."

"This is one summer festival that I know my sisters and I will never forget," Alice admitted softly. "Thank you, Pastor Thompson, for making it so memorable for all of us."

Everyone enjoyed the party. The Holzmanns had brought back many wonderful stories about their vacation in Europe, and the events of the wonderful day were discussed with delight. As the hour grew late, Lloyd took Ethel home, gallantly promising to return for her nieces in a few minutes. Joseph and Rachel, still adjusting to the time change from crossing the Atlantic, soon followed.

A soft summer rain began to fall outside as Alice carefully repacked the vases in the gift box.

"Pastor, thank you again for a lovely surprise." Alice saw

he was struggling into his coat and frowned. "You don't have to walk us home, you know, Lloyd will be escorting us back to the inn."

"Well, I'm sure that Lloyd will take good care of you, but I think Henry and Patsy have had enough celebration for one night." Kenneth smiled at the couple.

"I'm sorry?" Alice was confused.

"I know I could dance and sing until dawn," Patsy said. "We're just thrilled that we'll be staying here in Acorn Hill."

"Are you?" Jane said. "You mean, you are? That's terrific." She gave them both a hug. "When did this happen? Where are you going to live?"

"Right here," Patsy told her, and gave Kenneth a big smile. "Thanks to Pastor Thompson."

"You're going to live with Pastor Thompson?"

"No, but P-Pastor Thompson has g-g-given us the r-rectory," Henry told the sisters. "We'll b-b-be living here n-now."

"He has?" Louise blinked.

"Fred did a wonderful job restoring the rectory," Kenneth responded, "but it's really too big for a bachelor. Henry and Patsy will make far better use of it, and I'll still have access to an office here, with a separate entrance so I won't disturb them with my comings and goings."

"But where will you live?" Jane asked.

"The Holzmanns have a loft apartment above their shop that they've leased to me." Kenneth nodded in the direction of Acorn Hill Antiques. "I moved in last week."

"So that's why you had keys and were locking up the antique shop this morning," Jane said, wagging her finger gently.

"Is the apartment big?" Alice wanted to know. "Is there anything you need?"

"No, the Holzmanns have furnished it for me, and being right over an antique shop, I already feel right at home."

At her blank look he added, "My parents are antique dealers, too."

"Thank y-you again, Pastor," Henry said, and shook hands with Kenneth.

"You're very welcome." He smiled and nodded to the ladies. "Goodnight, and I look forward to seeing you all in church on Sunday."

When Lloyd returned, the three sisters walked home to Grace Chapel Inn. They were tired but happy. The new minister's kindness and generosity in giving up his new home for the Leys only emphasized what they already had discovered about Kenneth Thompson—that he was more like Daniel Howard than anyone could have imagined.

"We really did find the perfect minister," Alice murmured. "Didn't we?"

"Yes, we did," Louise said, putting an arm around her sister. "And there is no better place for a minister like Kenneth Thompson than right here in Acorn Hill."

Strawberry Popovers with Yogurt Sauce

Popovers
>4 eggs
>2 cups milk
>2 cups all-purpose flour
>¼ teaspoon salt
>¼ cup unsalted butter (melted)
>Fresh strawberries (about a pint),
>   finely diced
>(Other fruit can be substituted, such
>   as blueberries or cranberries)

Preheat oven to 425 degrees. In a large bowl, whisk eggs and milk together. Gradually add flour and salt, and whisk until smooth. Brush a twelve-count muffin tin with melted butter, then fill half full with batter. Sprinkle diced strawberries on top of batter. Bake for twenty to twenty-five minutes or until popped and golden brown.

Yogurt Sauce
>1 cup powdered sugar
>½ cup plain yogurt
>½ teaspoon vanilla extract
>Milk

Blend sugar, yogurt and vanilla extract in a small bowl. Add a tablespoon of milk if needed to thin to glaze consistency. Drizzle over warm popovers and serve immediately.

About the Author

Faith, family and humor have always been the strong foundation in Rebecca Kelly's life, which is constantly busy but never dull. Encouraged by her mother Joan, a popular local Christian humorist and speaker, Rebecca wrote her first book at age thirteen and hasn't stopped writing since.

When she's not writing or being a mom, Rebecca volunteers for a variety of church projects, including providing aid to the homeless and families in distress. She regularly gives writing workshops to area elementary school students and moderates a weekly writing discussion group on the Internet. An avid quilt maker and conservationist, Rebecca's most unusual hobby is uncovering "hidden" quilts, which are nineteenth-century quilts that have been used as batting for newer quilts. She has restored more than fifty to their former glory.

Rebecca presently resides in Florida with her two youngest children.

A Note from the Editors

∞

This original Guideposts Book was created by the Books and Inspirational Media Division of the company that publishes *Guideposts,* a monthly magazine filled with true stories of hope and inspiration.

Guideposts is available by subscription. All you have to do is write to Guideposts, 39 Seminary Hill Road, Carmel, New York 10512. When you subscribe, each month you can count on receiving exciting new evidence of God's presence, His guidance and His limitless love for all of us.

Guideposts Books are available on the World Wide Web at www.guidepostsbooks.com. Follow our popular book of devotionals, *Daily Guideposts,* and read excerpts from some of our best-selling books. You can also send prayer requests to our Monday morning Prayer Fellowship and read stories from recent issues of our magazines, *Guideposts, Angels on Earth,* and *Guideposts for Teens.*